A GAME CHANGER

NIKKY KAYE

ZACH

*W*inning was the best feeling in the world—whether it was on the football field or in bed. Right now, I was still basking in the glory of a truly epic *win*. And it was the off-season.

Someone stirred beside me and I groaned, reaching a hand to yank her back to bed. I heard the soft giggle as I snuggled closer to her, breathing in the scent of whoever this girl was. When I reached out to snake my arms around her waist, she squirmed under my touch.

"You're so sexy, Zach," she whispered, leaning closer to me.

It wasn't exactly poetry, but I hadn't brought her to my room for her huge… brain. She kissed me with such heated intensity that I couldn't repress my grin.

"Was I good?" It was a rhetorical question, but I wasn't above soliciting a little ego-stroking. Hell, I liked a *lot* of ego-stroking.

"The best," she murmured, shifting herself to straddle me. I moaned when she arched against me, leaning in to kiss me again when my phone rang.

"Fuck. Ignore it, baby," I muttered, reaching for her face and guiding it to mine.

But the stupid thing continued to ring and the more we tried to ignore it, the louder it seemed to get. With a growl of frustration, I grabbed the phone.

"Hello?"

"Zach, I'm sorry for, uh, waking you, but this is really important." My assistant's voice was polite, as it always was. But there was something in his tone that set the hair on my arms on end.

"Anderson, this better be good because I'll fire you if it isn't," I growled into the phone. The laughter of the pretty blonde straddling me vibrated through my groin, and I threw her a smirk.

"Zach, I think you need to go to Denver. I've booked your flight. It leaves in an hour, so you'd better hurry." Anderson said.

My eyebrows furrowed and I motioned for the girl to get off of me.

"What the hell is going on, Anderson?"

A long sigh came over the line. "Something happened to Dean and Margaret."

My stomach dropped. My insides churned as I swung my legs around and planted my feet on the floor. I wedged the phone between my shoulder and ear as I grabbed my jeans from the floor and pulled them on.

I walked to the floor to ceiling window in my highrise condo. When I looked out at the view of Tampa, I told myself that the weakness in my knees was due to the diligent work ethic of the blonde. I startled when I felt her arms wrapping around my waist.

"Give me a minute, Anderson," I mumbled and then placed my hand to cover the phone before turning to the groupie. Her sexy pout was souring. "I had fun last night, but I have a busy day ahead of me."

She frowned. "That's it? You're not even getting my number?"

I simply shrugged and returned my attention to the phone call. When she let out a dramatic huff, I glanced back to see her putting on her clothes. Fun time was over. It was going to end anyhow, though—what had she expected?

"What happened to Dean and Margaret?" I demanded.

Again, I heard Anderson sigh. "They got into an accident. Payton's also in the hospital but she's okay. Dean's in critical condition and Maggie... Maggie's gone."

I leaned forward, my forehead hitting the cool glass of the window. "Shit."

My eyes closing, my mind immediately flashed to an image of my beautiful and wonderful sister-in-law. I'd known her since she and Dean began to date in their junior year of high school. She became the mother figure I needed when our mother died of cancer and had been my shoulder to cry on when our father died a year after.

That was the worst time of my life. Until now.

"I'll see you at the airport, Anderson. You're coming with me. I'll be there as fast as I can."

I rinsed off, changed and then stuffed all my clothes in my duffel bag. It was only when I was in the cab heading to the airport that I realized I hadn't stopped to let Coach or the manager know I was leaving.

"I took care of that," Anderson assured me as we boarded the plane.

I gave him a curt nod, too distracted by my own fear to even say "thank you." Hopefully he understood. I was practically vibrating with anxiety for the entire flight. Usually that was Anderson's thing. When we finally arrived in Denver, we headed straight to the hospital, our bags slung over our shoulders.

The triage nurse in the Emergency Room wasn't impressed by my celebrity, or the fact that I'd bypassed the line of sick and injured people. "Sir, you have to—"

Fuck waiting. "Dean Pennington, I'm here for Dean Pennington. They were in an accident." My hand shook as I rubbed my forehead.

"Are you related to the patient, sir?"

"I'm his brother!" I almost shouted.

It took another ten minutes and the threat of a security guard intervention to locate Dean in the ICU. I didn't even know where the fuck that was, but I ran up the stairs, doubling my speed and ignoring Anderson shouting at me to slow down. Eventually I had to wait for him, because he knew where to go and I didn't.

At the fifth floor, I burst into the bubble of Intensive Care, and jogged past glass walls, searching for my brother's smile. His hair. *Anything.* I couldn't see shit, but something made me stop in front of a room with a lot of activity.

"What's going on?" I asked someone rushing in.

But he only shook his head. "Check in at the desk."

I tried to stop someone else. "Can you tell me where Dean Pennington is?"

But she didn't even stop to answer me, she just plowed past me.

My assistant appeared at my side, breathless from running up the stairs. "Zach…"

I shook my head. "It's not Dean. It can't be Dean. He won't leave Payton."

Anderson patted my shoulder, and I let him steer me to a chair while he talked to someone at the desk at the heart of the unit. My stomach flipped as I noticed the clerk and Anderson both looking pointedly at the room six feet away, full of medical personnel.

An eternity later, a doctor and some nurses piled out of the room. I jumped up. "Doctor, Dean Pennington?"

He paused. "Are you a relative?"

"I'm his brother."

The doctor sighed, his eyes red and tired-looking behind his thick glasses. "Let's talk."

He ushered me over to a tiny room off the hallway near the doors to the ICU. There was nothing hopeful about the look on his face, or the tiny fucking room with some flower paintings on the walls.

"Dean arrived here five hours ago with multiple injuries from an MVA."

I stared at him blankly.

"Multiple vehicle accident," he explained. "It was pretty serious. His wife died on impact."

I nodded. "I know." *Jesus, I was going to have to call Maggie's parents, wasn't I?* "Is Dean going to be okay?" I asked, my voice cracking.

Something in me already knew, but the extra pause the doctor took before answering was like the proverbial nail in the coffin. *Shit, bad analogy.*

With sorrowful eyes, he said, "I'm sorry. We did everything we could, but his injuries were just too severe." He waited, maybe wondering if I had follow-up questions.

I didn't.

"I'm very sorry for your loss. Dean was a good guy."

I blinked, not quite processing everything he'd said. "You knew him?"

"My daughter plays soccer with Payton."

"Payton." My heart stopped.

"She's okay. I was just with her in Pediatrics before I got paged back up here."

I ran a hand through my hair. "I should…"

"You should go see her. She needs a familiar face right now."

Familiar? How could anything be familiar again? Everything was different, now.

I couldn't even feel my fingertip when I punched the button to call the elevator. As I headed to Payton, a million memories flashed through my mind.

Who was I supposed to spend Thanksgiving now that they were gone, or Christmas and New Year's? I didn't have a family anymore because like Mom and Dad, Dean and Maggie were gone too.

The numbness in my body was suddenly pierced by jagged pain as I opened the door of my niece's room. Payton was fast asleep in the big, white hospital bed, unaware that she had just become an orphan in a span of a few hours. I closed my eyes as I sat on the molded plastic chair beside her bed and took her hand in mine.

Tears finally began falling from my eyes, which I quickly swiped away with the back of my free hand as fast as they were falling. As I took a deep breath—okay, I sniffled—Payton's eyes slowly opened.

"Uncle Zach?"

Cue more fucking tears that I didn't want her to see. I tried to smile. "Hey, sweets."

"Where's Mommy and Daddy?"

She looked at me with big brown eyes, innocence shining within them. It killed me that the light there was about to be extinguished forever. I bowed my head. How was I supposed to…? She didn't deserve this kind of heartbreak at such a young age.

A knock on the door saved me from breaking the news to her. I stood up when a tall woman came in the room wearing a formal suit.

"Hello, Mr. Pennington, I'm Lisa Simmons. I'm a social worker with the hospital. Can I have a word with you?"

I glanced down at Payton.

"Alone," she added.

I nodded, then leaned over and kissed Payton's forehead. "I'll be back in a bit, okay?"

As I followed the social worker out of the room, I realized I had no clue where Anderson was. I could've sworn he'd followed me into Payton's room but now he was nowhere in sight.

Miss Simmons cleared her throat beside me, forcing me to refocus my attention. "I'm very sorry for your loss, Mr. Pennington. But there are some matters that need to be discussed sooner rather than later."

"I can pay for everything," I said. Did she seriously want to settle the hospital bill now?

She shook her head. "I've contacted your brother's lawyer and asked about Payton. He would settle all of this with you in person but he's currently out of the city right now. He'll be here tomorrow to inform you of everything regarding the estate."

Of course, Dean and Maggie would have a will. He was the responsible one. The only will I had was the one that stubbornly led me to make poor decisions.

"Can you just get to the point?" I asked. "I have a niece in there who needs me."

She nodded. "I understand that, sir, and again I'm sorry for your loss. But we're talking about your niece here—about who will have custody of her."

"What about Maggie's family?"

The social worker shook her head. "According to your brother's lawyer, if anything happens to either him or Maggie or to the both of them, they didn't want her to have to leave her home."

My mind tried to put the pieces together. "Maggie's parents live in New Zealand. And so does the rest of Maggie's family," I stated, not sure where this conversation was heading.

"Your brother and his wife listed you as Payton's legal guardian should anything happen to them," she said, her voice gentle.

I could only stare at her. "What?" Had Dean talked to me about this? I sagged against the wall in the hallway.

"You'll have to discuss the specifics of the estate with the lawyer, but based on the paperwork he faxed to us, the hospital can discharge Payton into your care tomorrow. She's to stay for observation tonight."

"My entire life is in Florida," I argued. "And Dean knows I have no clue how to raise a child." *Knew.* I had to remind myself that my brother was in past tense, here. I squeezed my eyes shut and took a deep breath.

"You can always transfer here. I'm sure your management can arrange something," she said, then her tone turned more officious. "The alternative is that she's transferred into the care of DCFS. Obviously, if there is a capable, available family member, the preference is for the child to be placed with them."

I groaned and slid down the wall into a squatting position as I tried to make sense of what had happened in the span of a few hours since I had woken up.

My brother was dead. My sister-in-law was dead. And I had to move to Denver to take care of their five-year old daughter.

"Zach?"

I looked up and saw Anderson. "Where the hell have you been?"

He kneeled down beside me and handed me a bag. "We needed to eat so I went to look for the nearest Subway."

I shook my head. "I'm not hungry. But I'll take the bag for throwing up into," I joked. *Sort of.*

"So, what's going to happen now? When do you want to have the funeral?"

"What?"

Anderson sighed, stuffing his sandwich back in the bag as he turned to look at me. "Zach, your brother and his wife are dead. They need to be buried. You need to get the two of them into caskets and make sure that they have a proper funeral. Prepare a eulogy."

I closed my eyes, unable to comprehend any more of what Anderson had to say.

First, I was told that my brother was in critical condition and that Maggie was dead.

Second, I find out that Dean was dead too.

Third, I had to raise my niece.

And now, I have to plan a funeral. What the hell? I looked at my assistant, who also happened to be the only real friend I had.

"I have to take Payton," I said dully.

That made Anderson pause. "What? Take her where?"

"Dean and Maggie want me to raise their five-year old daughter, apparently." The proposal still had me reeling.

He patted my knee. "You'll figure this out."

I stood up, shaking my head. "No. *You'll* figure this out." Something inside me hardened, like a protective shell around my preferred reality.

"Um, sorry?"

"Find me a nanny for her, Anderson. Someone who's qualified to raise a child. Because we both know that I will fail on that aspect."

Anderson nodded, his expression grim. "Duly noted. I'll do that the moment we settle in our hotel rooms. I've already gotten each of us a place to stay. I think we'll be here for two to five days, depending on when you'll hold that funeral."

I didn't have the heart to tell him right then that I was expected to stay in Denver for more than a few days —like, ten to fifteen years.

I rubbed my forehead. "I don't even know how I'm supposed to break the news down to Payton."

"You could ask a doctor to do it and then just be by her side when she cries."

I shook my head and sighed. "I'll think of something." I was about to ask him to call Maggie's family, but realized that I needed to do that. There was only so much I could delegate without being a complete asshole.

"Can you tell Coach that I need to switch teams?"

Anderson gaped at me. "Dude!"

Right, that was another thing I should probably do

myself. I groaned at the prospect of getting my ass chewed out and probably involving the Player's Association, as well. *Fuck my life.*

"I don't really have much of a choice. It's either I move here or she's in foster care. I can't do that to Payton." Not to mention that Dean and Maggie would haunt me for the rest of my days.

My footsteps heavy, I headed back to Payton's room to find her watching TV. I sat beside her and smiled at her softly, reaching out to tuck her silky brown hair behind her ear.

Her eyes were wide and hopeful when she looked at me. "Did the lady tell you where Mommy and Daddy are?"

"Payton, sweets, do you remember what your Daddy told you about Grandma and Grandpa?"

She nodded her head slowly. "He told me that they're in heaven, happy and watching over us. They're our angels."

"I think we gained more angels, sweets," I whispered, taking her hand. "I'm so sorry, Payton, but they're gone. They're with Grandma and Grandpa now."

If I thought I'd been hurting before, I was wrong. Nothing shattered me more than seeing my niece's heart break in front of my eyes.

She thrashed in her bed and screamed, telling me that this wasn't a good joke. When she asked me why, I had no answer to offer.

Payton wailed in agony as I restrained her, hugging her as tightly as I could. Her face was wet against my shirt, and tears dripped from my jaw as we cried together.

We'd both just lost our family. We only had each other, now.

It was only then it occurred to me why Dean had chosen me to be her guardian—because he trusted that I would know exactly what to do.

Except, I didn't have the first goddamn clue.

EMMA

I'd been waiting for an opening for work since the day I handed my application to the agency and they promised me that I would be contacted the following week. Two weeks later, I could practically see my phone collecting dust where it sat on the thrift store table I'd shoved against the farthest wall of my cramped apartment.

When the agency finally called, I was beyond thrilled. It was a rush interview request, at the most extravagant hotel in Denver. I was too relieved to ask questions or even think twice. I immediately agreed, not even bothering to ask why the interview was at a hotel.

I arrived ten minutes early, looking as presentable as my secondhand wardrobe could make me. I didn't have money to buy myself new clothes, but I'd managed to scavenge a plain black sleeveless dress and topped it off with a gray cardigan. I braided my dark hair, applied a small amount of makeup on my face, and hoped that I could charm my employer enough to make them hire me.

As directed, I went straight up to room 708 and I rang the buzzer next to the door. A moment later, the door swung open to reveal the most gorgeous man I'd ever laid eyes on.

His dark hair was short and tousled—like he'd just rolled out of bed—and the scruff of beard on his chiseled jaw made me swallow hard. So did the way his black t-shirt stretched over his chest. His brown eyes bore into mine and his eyebrows furrowed in confusion.

"Hello," he said, his voice deep. *Holy smokes, this guy.*

I blinked. "Hi. I'm Emma Smith."

Like a veil lifting, his eyes filled with clarity and his lips curled into a smile. He opened his door, beckoning me inside.

I was hit by his masculine scent the moment I entered his hotel room. I looked around, noting how clean and neat it was, aside from the one suitcase with rumpled clothes thrown on top. I searched for toys or kid stuff but saw nothing. Nor did I see a woman's things, leaving me to wonder where his wife or partner was.

I frowned. For the first sixty seconds of a job interview, I already had too many questions.

He cleared his throat and I turned around to find him sprawled on the bed, his chest bare and a sexy smirk on his face.

My mouth almost dropped at the sight of my possible future boss looking like he was posing for a sexy calendar. And when did he lose the shirt?

He chuckled and I knew it was mostly because I resembled a frightened animal. "Look, I don't know how you found out I'm here in Denver. I don't even know how you found my hotel room and I'm not sure whether or not I should be flattered or scared by your stalking skills, but *I know* why you came here."

For the interview.

He knew about the interview so why did he look like he was ready to devour me? I couldn't speak, completely stunned at what was going on. And stalking him? What was that about?

He continued to speak. "But I'll wrap my mind about that later. You came at the perfect time, so what the hell are you waiting for?"

"What?"

He laughed. He actually laughed. "Strip."

Did he just...

"What?" I blurted out.

He sat up and I could actually see the bulge forming in his pants. I looked away like my eyes were on fire, but he'd already seen me glance at it and he laughed even more. "Baby, I like role play on most days but today I just want a release."

Oh hell, no. Did this guy...? "Er, I think I might be in the wrong room."

His eyebrows shot up in surprise. "What are you talking about?"

"I'm supposed to be here for an interview," I said and then motioned to his—*him*. "Not... that." As though *'that'* could be conveyed with a flap of my hand.

His eyes narrowed. "Interview for what?"

I chewed on my bottom lip and replied, "I'm the nanny."

"Shit." He got off the bed, held up a hand and said, "One moment." He grabbed his phone and headed outside at the small balcony that his room offered.

I just stood there, completely dumbfounded at what

was going on. I was not the kind of girl that men came on to like that. I didn't have bedroom eyes like this man did. I barely had living room eyes.

After two minutes he came back, flushed and with his head bowed.

"I'm so sorry," he said. "I don't know what came over me. Well, actually, I do, but I should've asked properly."

I looked down at my plain dress and worn purse, wondering what about me had prompted such an invitation. I thought I looked presentable, not... "It's fine. I should've just said it the moment you opened your door."

"Could we have a do-over?" he asked. I nodded. He exhaled loudly and ran a hand through his hair. "I'm Zach Pennington."

I smiled and stuck out my hand for him to shake. "I'm Emma Smith and I'm the new nanny for your little girl." I glanced around the sparse hotel room again. "Is she with her mom right now?"

Something flashed in his eyes and he turned away. "Payton's not here but we can go see her. Could you just give me five minutes to get ready? Have you eaten? You can order room service for breakfast. Anything you want."

He was nice when he wasn't propositioning me, I had to give him that.

I politely declined and sat on the couch as I waited for him to get ready. He was done in just a few minutes and he rushed me out of the room. "I'll explain everything in the car."

"Where are we going?"

"To the hospital," he answered once the two of us were settled in his car.

The hospital? Was his daughter a patient? I tried to sit on my confusion and curiosity and waited for him to explain.

He looked at me and smiled apologetically. "I'm really sorry about earlier... Emma, right? Is it okay if I call you Emma?"

"Sure." With those lips he could call me anything he wanted, and I'd come.

Zach Pennington had a charming blush, as well as dimples to die for. "I feel really bad about the whole, um, misunderstanding."

Presumably he meant the part where he expected me to jump on his lap—which would probably not feel bad at all. I shook my head. "It's fine. So where is... Payton? With your wife?"

"I don't have a wife."

I wasn't supposed to be happy with his answer. This sexy, gorgeous man didn't have a wife. But then again, maybe Payton's mother was his girlfriend or something like that. Still, the thought that he could be single woke up the butterflies in the pit of my stomach.

"Payton's my niece," he began and my eyebrows rose in surprise. "Her parents..." He sighed. "My brother and sister-in-law died in a car accident on Sunday."

Holy moly.

I wasn't expecting that.

Zach stopped the car at a red light and turned to me with a solemn look. He ran a hand through his wet hair, combing through it as he waited for me to reply.

I swallowed hard. "Was she...?"

"She was in the car with them, but she's okay. Drunk driver. Car's a total write-off. It's a miracle that Payton's okay." He looked back at the now-green light and gave a bitter kind of chuckle. "Relatively speaking," he added.

My mind flashed back to when I was six and was in the car with my Dad. I'd loved driving with my father in his taxi, listening to music and reading street signs. It was just him and me, since my mother had died giving birth to me. Yeah, apparently that doesn't just happen in old books.

When he was killed by a fare, the community went into shock but it *broke* me. After that, my life was a series of foster homes until I aged out. The day you turn eighteen, something magical happens and you're able to be an adult and fend for yourself.

At least, that's the theory.

"—live in Florida," Zach was saying, and I turned my attention back to him. "But I'm going to have to arrange to move here, now." He winced, as though the idea was painful.

"You're taking custody of her?" I asked.

"It was what they wanted." He shrugged, but I doubted it was that easy to contemplate. "Something similar happened to us when we were younger. Dean was the one who practically raised me," he said quietly. His eyes were fixed on the road but I could see the tears that he tried to keep at bay.

"I'm sorry. Couldn't you take her to Florida?" As soon as I said it I wanted to kick myself. *Way to lose the job before you get it, Emma.*

"She needs to stay in her own home, around familiar things and people."

I nodded.

"The problem is," Zach said, his hands tightening on the steering wheel, "I don't have a parental bone in my body and I'm always working, which is why I hired you."

The word 'hired' made my ears perk up. So did the word 'bone' but I focused on the job part of his statement. I straightened in my seat. "I'm hired? But you haven't asked me any questions."

"You seem nice," he said with a small smile. "Like the kind of woman that Maggie would have approved of. My assistant says that the agency is top notch and has the best people, and I'm paying them a small fortune, so…"

His assistant? This man was so confusing. One minute it was like he wanted to hold his niece like she was a crystal flower and the next minute he was delegating everything, as though she were a temporary inconvenience.

"I see," I said slowly, unsure how I felt about this.

"Also, I really am sorry about earlier, so I thought it'd be better to skip the formal interview and just hire you on the spot."

"Oh. Okay. Thanks?"

He glanced over at me. "That is, if you still want the job?"

"Yes!"

"Okay, then." A smile tugged at his mouth.

"Okay, then!" I almost hugged him but refrained from doing so, immediately remembering that he was my boss and that it was completely unprofessional. "Oh my gosh, thank you so much. I'm going to love that kid like my own."

His eyebrows rose as he stopped again for a red light.

"You haven't even met her yet. You might change your mind."

"I'm good with kids."

"Good quality for a nanny," Zach said with a chuckle.

I didn't think that Payton would be a tough kid. She was going through a lot of hard emotions right now, but I felt fairly confident that I could help her since I went through it too. "Nah, I'm sure I'll be fine."

Zach quirked a smile. "Confident. I like it. Oh, do you mind if we make a quick stop? I promised to get Payton a teddy bear last night, and the ones at the hospital gift shop suck."

Awww. "Not at all."

I bit my lip to stop myself from smiling. My lips kept curving up in spite of my efforts as we parked at a big box store and headed inside.

"What's she like?" I asked as Zach scoured the toy section for a very particular bear.

He shrugged. "Cute. Smart. Beautiful. She's the sweetest kid I've ever met, but my opinion might be biased since I'm her uncle. Plus, I'm not exactly around a lot of kids."

He kept going on and on about how amazing Payton was and as he did, my interest in meeting the little girl continued to build. By the time we finally arrived at the hospital, I was nearly giddy with excitement.

I wasn't the only one, though.

It was impossible not to notice how everyone greeted Zach. Blushes and coy smiles from women and broad grins and high fives from the guys. A few people stopped him for a picture, to which he surrendered without protest.

Was he a celebrity?

From bits and pieces of conversations he had with people, I came to conclude that Zach must be some kind of professional athlete. The questions were piling up in my mind, but they would have to wait until later.

He stopped at a door and turned to me, his face almost entirely covered by the giant teddy bear. "I'm not sure how she is right now," he said to me from behind the bear's head. "Anderson's already here and he texted me that Payton hasn't been talking. She's upset, so I'm not totally sure how to tell her that I got her a nanny."

"Let me do my magic then," I said, trying to sound self-assured. Assuring.

He paused for a moment as he looked at me carefully. Whatever he was searching for in my face, he found. The butterflies rose in my belly again.

"Okay," he said, then opened the door and stepped inside. "Hi sweets, look what I got you."

When I stepped into the room, I saw a little girl almost swallowed up by the huge hospital bed. She looked small and weak and looked like she just woke up crying. My heart broke at the sight of her and I watched as Zach moved closer and handed her the bear.

She reached out to touch it, and as her little fingers smoothed over the fake fur her eyes welled up.

"Daddy told me he'd get me a big bear for my birthday," Payton said softly and then broke down crying.

Zach stood in front of her, completely speechless. He obviously had no clue how to comfort the little girl.

Show time for Mary Poppins.

I moved forward and pushed him aside gently. I sat on the bed and touched Payton's shoulder. "Hi, Payton."

She looked up, her big brown eyes brimming with tears. "Who are you?"

"My name's Emma," I said softly and I touched the big bear beside her, "Did your uncle get this for you? Wow, it's so pretty."

"Daddy was supposed to get it for me." Her tone was forlorn, not sullen.

"Your daddy told your uncle, I'm sure."

"I'd rather have Daddy here than this bear."

For a moment I was surprised that the pieces of my heart made no sound as they shattered on the linoleum floor. I reached out and pulled her in my arms for a careful hug. I didn't want to overwhelm her, but the compulsion to hold her was impossible to overcome.

"I'm sure he'd rather be here in person, too. But your daddy's still here, sweetheart. So is your mommy. They're in your heart, aren't they?"

"But I'm never gonna see them, ever again."

"Every time you think of them, they're with you. Did your Mom and Dad ever tell you what you were made of?"

Her lip trembled. "Sugar and spice and something nice?"

Zach gave a strangled laugh behind me. "No, sweets."

"Half of you is your mom and half of you is your dad. So you see, they'll never leave you."

"Which part is *me*, then?"

"All of you," I said.

Payton frowned.

"Do you like Oreos?" I asked. *Rhetorical question, right?*

"Well, you're like the cream in the middle of an Oreo. The cookie can't exist without you holding the other parts together."

She nodded, as if my weird analogy made sense. *Thank god.*

I pulled away from her slightly and reached for a tissue on the little hospital tray table. "Now, I hate to see that pretty face crying. Your mommy and daddy would hate to see you sad."

"Then they shouldn't have died!" She sniffled with a giant snorking sound and glared at me. "They… broke my cookie!"

"Aw, hell," Zach mumbled. "You're killing me, smalls."

"Sometimes things happen that we don't want to, but that doesn't mean that we meant for it to happen," I began to explain, repeating the words one of my foster parents once told me when I had broken down in their house when I was younger. "And that doesn't mean that our lives are gonna stop because it happened."

I pointed at Zach. "You still have your uncle. There are some who have none. I didn't have an uncle."

Payton looked at me with pity. Her sobs had turned into sniffles as she snuggled closer to me. "Who are you again? I forgot."

"I'm Emma," I told her and kissed the top of her head, "And I'll be helping your uncle take care of you."

She nodded her head as she hugged me tightly. "I don't think Uncle Zach would do a good job taking care of me by himself," she whispered confidentially in my ear.

I giggled and turned to Zach, who had sank on a chair and looked at us incredulously. I played with

Payton for a while until Zach stood up and motioned for me to go outside with him. I turned back to Payton and told her that I'd be back soon; there was just something I had to discuss with her uncle.

"So, what do you think?" Zach asked as we took a seat in the waiting room.

"What do you mean?"

He shrugged. "Payton."

"She's wonderful."

"You were great with her earlier. Knew the right words."

I smiled and looked away. "Let's just say I had someone say something similar to me."

"You were an orphan?"

"*Were?*" I tamped down the acid tone of my laugh as I looked into Zach's warm brown eyes. "It's not really something you grow out of. Yes, I'm still an orphan. I only had my Dad and after he died I went into care. I wasn't lying when I said I didn't have an uncle, or anyone else who could take me. Payton's lucky to have you."

"Is that why you wanted to be a nanny?" He looked genuinely interested.

I sighed. "To be honest, I wasn't expecting to nanny an orphaned girl. But I guess the reason I fell into this situation is because I know how to handle her."

"So, you're okay with all of this?" Zach asked, his eyes turning serious. "Because I really need your help with her. When the season starts I'll be all over the place, not to mention training. I can't squeeze taking care of a child into my schedule."

His words took me aback. Just when I thought he honestly cared about his niece, she didn't compare to his job with balls or sticks or whatever the hell he did. Though I suddenly rankled with resentment, I had to push it down.

Payton needed someone to take care of her the way a parent could. I might not be her mother, but I knew what it was like to need a parental figure. It would be better as a team effort, though I got the feeling already that I wouldn't be able to depend on Zach for bedtime stories and cutting up dinosaur-shaped chicken nuggets.

My chin rose, my body stiffening as though I was wearing a suit of armor.

"I'll take care of her like she's my own, Mr. Pennington."

ZACH

*T*he shrill ring of my alarm clock woke me up. I groaned and rolled then fell off the tiny bed that I slept on in Dean's guest room. At six and a half feet and 250 pounds I found most beds constraining, and this was no exception. Annoyed, I reached for my phone and sent Anderson a text order for a new bed for me, one big enough to use as a life raft.

As much as I loved my brother, I hated the fact that he had refused my offer to buy him a better—*bigger*— house. I'd offered it as a birthday gift or even as a thank you gift since he had practically raised me on his own, but he declined, telling me that it was only the three of them; they didn't need a bigger space to live in.

Now it was only me and Payton, and even if the house was big enough for Dean and Maggie it sure as hell wasn't enough for me.

I heard knocking on my door and knew it was Payton.

I opened the door and plastered with a big smile for my niece. The last thing she needed to see was how unhappy I was with the situation. I didn't want her to think that she was a burden to me.

Technically she was, but she didn't need to know that.

Payton smiled back at me and handed me my toothbrush. I chuckled and followed her to the main bathroom located between her room and mine.

Payton and I had developed a routine after the funeral and after I officially moved in. We'd brush our teeth together and then she'd leave so I could take a shower and then right after I was done, we'd have breakfast together. Emma would arrive at seven thirty and then Payton would take her bath with the help of her nanny.

"We don't have milk," Payton announced once I filled our bowls. "I don't like dry cereal."

While she pouted I ran a hand through my wet hair, not knowing how I was supposed to respond. What was the right parental response here—make something else? Tell her to eat it dry? I was freshly showered and hungry. Now, without milk, I was disappointed, too—but so was my snack-sized roommate.

"I'll have Anderson go grocery shopping later."

Payton pursed her lips but nodded, sitting on her spot at the table. She played with her breakfast as I practically shoveled mine into my mouth.

"How did you sleep?" I asked her after gulping down a glass of milk.

She looked up at me then shrugged. "The same. No nightmares." There was relief in her big brown eyes.

Thank god.

The first night after I officially moved in, Payton woke up screaming in the middle of the night.

I didn't like it. Her panic put me on edge and brought back a wave of bad memories that I'd buried in the back of my mind. She'd been screaming and thrashing in her bed when I found her, and I had to shake her awake and comfort her until she stopped crying and fell back asleep.

The doorbell rang and Payton squealed as she rushed to the front door to open it for Emma. The two of them waltzed back in the kitchen, hand in hand, while Payton let Emma know about the milk situation. *Little snitch.*

I leaned against the counter, allowing myself a moment to check out Emma. She was just too pretty to ignore.

Her worn jeans hugged her hips and thighs alluringly, and her t-shirt looked like it might have gotten shrunk in the wash, because her midriff was exposed when she leaned over to whisper something in Payton's ear.

Not for the first time, I had to push down my attraction to her. My job was to tuck my niece into bed, not the nanny. *Keep your eye on the ball, Pennington,* I told myself. But my balls weren't the only ones itching for practice time.

Emma greeted me with a smile before ushering Payton upstairs to clean up and get dressed. I watched the two of them leave, grateful for the fact that Payton liked her and that they got along well. It had only been a couple of weeks, but Emma and Payton were already thick as thieves.

I was still contemplating that tempting sliver of skin when they tromped back into the kitchen. Then I checked the time—*shit!*

"I'm outta here," I announced.

Payton rushed to me and gave me a big hug.

"Will you pick me up from art class today?" she asked, her gaze hopeful.

I glanced at Emma, who turned away. This had been a regular occurrence and every time she asked, I always told her I couldn't.

"Sorry, sweets, but you know how grueling my training can get. I don't think I can, but I'll have Anderson pick you up with ice cream."

Something flashed in her eyes but she nodded. "Okay, I guess. But tell him I want strawberry."

Emma cleared her throat purposefully.

"Strawberry, *please*," Payton added.

I kissed her forehead, inhaling the watermelon scent of her shampoo. "Be good for Emma, okay? I'll see you tonight."

Feeling as awkward as a teenager, I glanced at Emma. Every time I left, I didn't know what I was supposed to say to her. Today was no different.

I lifted up my hand to wave at her. "Uh, take care of her for me." *Lame.*

"Always," she replied with a reassuring smile and then shut the door, leaving me standing on the doorstep of the small bungalow I now called home.

New home, new work—and both of them were minefields that I was still learning how to tiptoe around.

The Denver Broncos had not greeted me with open arms and back slaps the moment I stepped foot on their field. It was high school all over again, where someone was judged on their looks, friends, or financial status. On paper I aced all those categories, but here I was beating my head against the mean girl clique. Everyone stared at me like I was an outcast. A few players looked as though they wanted to punch me in the throat.

I knew that they were treating me like a social pariah because I was once their competition. I was the guy who scored a touchdown and stole their glory last season, ruining their four-year championship streak. And now I was a part of their team.

We had an even bigger chance to win back the title now that I was a part of the team, but I also knew that they didn't like me enough to throw the ball my way or have me score a winning touchdown.

They'd rather lose their glory than give me mine.

Even Coach Matthews showed his distaste for me. He had me run laps, *just laps*, the first day I joined and as much as I loved running, I hated the fact that it was all I did. He didn't even let me join the practice. I wasn't a new player. I was merely a new addition to the team. I wasn't a rookie either. I've been playing professional football for two years. All the things Coach made me do were meant to make me look like a wuss.

"Hey, Pennington!" Matthews shouted, glaring at me.

I refrained from rolling my eyes at him. I knew it would just land me in more trouble. "Yes, Coach?"

"Run ten laps around the field. A hundred and fifty push-ups and then I'll see if you could join the proper practice. See if you're ready."

Was he seriously kidding me? Did he not see me score that touchdown six months ago? I bit my tongue and started running. I could hear the others snickering in my wake, amusement evident on all their faces.

By the end of the training session, I was completely pissed and fuming. Coach didn't let me join the practice again and even went as far as making me watch the others play while I sat on the bench. What made things worse, it was obvious that his play was a flop and his defenses were weak.

They obviously weren't going to steal the trophy back and as much as that thought satisfied me, the fact that I was now on the losing team irritated the hell out of me.

I called Anderson the moment I got back in my car. "Anderson, I need time off from Payton."

"What?" Anderson said. "What are you talking about?"

I honestly didn't know what I was talking about. All I knew was that I needed booze and girls to de-stress. "I need to go clubbing."

"But what about Payton?"

"Stay with her until I get home," I responded, heading to the house.

I didn't know Payton's exact schedule, but I knew that on Mondays, she had art class that ended at four. It was 3:30 in the afternoon at the moment and I knew they weren't home yet. Just a quick shower and change of clothes and I'd be ready to break out.

"But Emma's leaving at eight, Zach," Anderson reasoned. "You want me to stay with Payton until you come home, which is probably at the crack of dawn? She's your niece, your responsibility—not mine."

Fuck, he was whining a lot these days, considering how much I paid him. Then again, I did make him move to Denver.

"Just stay with her, Andy," I said, irritated that I was on the verge of begging. "She's not even supposed to be my responsibility."

With that, I ended the call. I didn't care how mean I

sounded with what I said. I just needed time off. After a quick shower and change of clothes, I was done before the clock struck four. Only losers and gigolos went started their evenings this early, but I didn't care. I'd welcome the Seniors' menu at the bar, if it came to that.

I just needed to… get out.

Google and Uber got me to the club that Dean had brought me to when I first came to Denver to see him and Maggie after they moved. That was six years ago. I hesitated outside the door for some unknown reason, before being jostled in by a trio of businessmen shaking off the day.

The bar hadn't changed that much. The only thing missing was… my brother. *Shit.*

"Hey, I know you," the bartender said, sliding me the beer I ordered, "You're the guy that scored the touchdown, the one who ruined the Broncos' streak."

I winced. I'd been getting that a lot since I moved here. "Yeah well, I'm part of the Broncos now so I'll steal that championship trophy back for you."

"Make sure that you do," the bartender stated.

I continued on drinking until the party scene finally came to life and the music turned up. Suddenly, people crowded the bar and there were people bringing down the dance floor. I finished my fifth bottle of beer before heading down, and soon found myself grinding against a redhead who seemed to be thrilled to have caught my attention. I knew she'd been trying to; I'd caught her glancing in my direction twice.

"I'm glad you've finally noticed me," she purred in my ear as she shimmied against me.

Without warning, her lips crashed on mine and the steam in the club skyrocketed.

It was hot, fast, hard, but I found myself a little distracted. I guess even being attacked by horny women loses its novelty after a while.

"Let's get out of here." She licked my lips as she said it.

I simply nodded. I'd wanted a break, right? This was like parole, a visit to the life I lived not that long ago. Somehow, though, it felt different. Almost… boring.

Regardless, I dragged her off of the dance floor and into a hallway that would lead us to the parking lot and the confines of my car. But just as we neared the exit, my phone rang and I groaned. The last time a phone call cockblocked me, I received the news about my brother.

"Ignore it," said the redhead.

"Just give me a minute," I murmured before fishing my phone from my pocket. I saw the screen flashing Emma's name. "Hello?"

I placed a finger against the girl's lips and she sucked my finger into her mouth. I stifled a groan as Emma began to talk.

"Payton's having a meltdown."

"Can't you calm her down?" I asked, trying to suppress a moan as the girl in front of me began unbuckling my pants.

"Andy and I have been trying. We wouldn't be calling you if we'd successfully calmed her down," Emma told me, the panic seeping in her voice. In the background of the call, I could hear high-pitched cries. "She's hysterical, Zach. She needs you."

Parole revoked.

"Fine. I'm coming home," I said, sighing as the girl in front of me managed to unzip my fly. "Babe, I think we'll have to continue this some other time. I'm needed somewhere."

She pouted prettily but stood up. She pulled out a pen from her purse and scribbled down her number on my forearm. Then she crashed her lips against mine, her tongue roaming my mouth for a moment before she pulled away. "I'll expect your call."

With a smirk, I got into my car and drove to the house. When I arrived at the small bungalow, I heard screaming. I rushed inside to find her on the ground, crying and screaming, and recoiling each time Emma or Anderson reached out to her.

"What the heck happened?" I asked the moment I stepped in.

Nobody responded. Payton seemed unaware of my arrival.

I moved closer to my niece, "Sweets, it's me. It's Uncle Zach."

When she registered that I was there she jerked away from me, too.

"You don't want me," she wailed. "You don't want to stay here with me but you don't have a choice."

My heart broke at her words. I'd said something similar to Dean after our parents' loss. *How the fuck did he hold it together?* I wondered now. My brother was always stronger than me, and every day I was reminded of it.

I knelt in front of Payton and looked her straight in the eye. "Sweets, it's me. It's Uncle Zach and I'm not leaving you. I want to stay with you. I want to take care of you. So do Emma and Anderson."

"You'll leave, too."

I reached out and touched her hand gently and then

moved to touch her face. I made sure our gazes were locked together. "I won't. I promise you I'll stay."

And slowly, like she finally believed me, Payton crawled closer and wrapped her small arms around my neck.

We stayed in that position, her face buried on my chest and my arms wrapped around her, until she fell asleep. I carried her to bed and Emma helped me tuck her in. I kissed her forehead gently and the two of us headed out of her room, gently closing the door behind us.

"What happened?" I demanded in a low voice.

Emma looked at me, her blue eyes tired. "I don't know! She was looking for you since we got home. When the clock turned eight, she wouldn't go to bed unless you were here. We finally convinced her but then she only slept for a little while before waking up with a night terror or something."

I ran a hand through my hair. "What do you think happened?"

"I think she thought you abandoned her," Emma said, honesty stinging in her words. "Look, Zach, I know it's not my place to criticize, but she needs you. Not just the food, clothing and shelter thing. You're the closest thing she's got to a parent."

"But I don't know how to be a parent! That was Dean's department. Not mine," I said, the frustration rising in my voice. "And I have a life too, Emma. I want to actually enjoy it."

"But she *needs* you," Emma urged, her blue eyes staring straight into my soul. "She's five years old, Zach."

Memories of Dean taking care of me spun through

my mind in an instant with such intensity it almost knocked me off my feet. Dean had always been there for me, even though he could've left me when he turned eighteen. And now I needed to be there for Payton.

"Fine, but on one condition," I said, looking at Emma. "I can't do this alone. I need you to move in with us. If I'm the closest thing she has to a dad, then you're the closest she has to a mother."

Something flashed in her eyes. Hesitation, maybe. What would I do if she said no? Payton needed me, right? Well, I needed Emma here to make my life easier.

Emma nodded her head. "Deal. For Payton."

"For Payton." I instinctively stuck out my hand to shake on it, but she crossed her arms over her chest.

Looked like my nanny was going to be the new warden.

I shouldn't have agreed with Zach.

It had been two days since I moved in with them. I didn't have my own bedroom and although Zach had offered the room he was staying in, I was more uncomfortable with that idea than the couch. Neither of us suggested that one of us make use of the master bedroom, which as far as I knew hadn't been touched since Zach's brother and sister-in-law died.

In any case, I was fine with sleeping on the pull-out and making the living room my bedroom at night. I'd lived in a lot of foster homes and some of them didn't offer me a room to sleep in. I knew how to share, and I also knew how to create my own space when needed.

But the lack of a bedroom wasn't what bothered me. What bothered me most was Zach Pennington himself. Since I moved in, he thought I had just relieved him from his responsibilities with Payton.

He'd been coming home at dawn since I moved in, smelling like sweat, cigarette smoke and perfume. It wasn't hard to figure out where he had been. I had to take care of his drunken ass and it suddenly felt like I was taking care of two kids and not just one.

I had to draw the line. The night before, he came home completely drunk—and he was loud when he was drunk. I was so scared that he'd wake Payton up and she would end up seeing her uncle at the state he was in. I didn't want to traumatize the little girl.

What was worse was that he vomited the moment he came in the house. I mean, really? He couldn't throw up in the bushes outside?

Then I had to wrestle him, fully clothed, into the shower to clean up. I debated whether or not to remove his clothes. The part of me that found him attractive— at pretty much *any* other time—was momentarily tempted, but the disgusted, infuriated, sopping wet part of me decided to throw him into his bed instead. Let him soak his own bedding, I thought.

It was only when I was cleaning up the front entry area that I realized I'd be the one doing his damn laundry, anyhow.

There was no way that I was letting this continue.

Just after seven in the morning, I gave up on trying to get back to sleep and dressed in jeans and a t-shirt. I knocked on Zach's bedroom door and then just barged in, knowing that he couldn't have locked it when I helped him to his bed because he was unconscious. I shook him awake.

He stirred and groaned, rolling on his bed. His clothes were damp and still a bit smelly, I noticed as he slowly opened his brown eyes. He stared at the ceiling and groaned again.

"Fuck." It was like a morning affirmation. He slowly sat up, holding his head. *Served him right.*

I rolled my eyes and handed him a glass of water and some ibuprofen. "Here."

He gave me a grateful but sheepish smile and took the medicine from my hand. I didn't return the smile as he downed it with the water. He set the glass down on his nightstand and then ran a hand through his tousled hair. "Payton's still asleep?"

"Yes," I answered and crossed my arms over my chest. "We need to talk, Zach."

He rubbed his eyes. "I'm not exactly in the right state of mind right now and I need to sober up for training."

"It's Sunday!" I said, unable to hide my exasperation. Was he going to keep this up when the season started? "Look, you know what, Zach? I'm done."

He furrowed his eyebrows. "What are you talking about?"

"I agreed to move in with you two because you needed my help and I did it for Payton," I began, "but since I moved in, you've practically left me to handle Payton and that's not fair, Zach. I'm the nanny and it's part of my job to take care of her but she's your responsibility, not mine."

"I'm not getting your point."

I stared at him. Was he still drunk or just this dense? "I'm trying to tell you that you're supposed to take care of her too! But you've been clubbing since I moved in and you come home drunk and *I* have to take care of you too!"

"I'll pay you double then."

I huffed and resisted the urge to scream at him. "You don't need to, I'm done."

"What do you mean you're done?" Zach asked, his

eyes widening with panic. He staggered to standing and winced. "You're not thinking of quitting, aren't you?"

"You're leaving?"

The tiny voice made both of us freeze.

I slowly turned around and saw Payton standing in the doorway, her eyes brimming with tears. She'd clearly just woke up. Her hair was a mess and she was carrying Zach's toothbrush along with hers. When the first tear tumbled down her cheek, my heart broke and Payton suddenly ran back to her room.

I chased after her, but she slammed the door in my face. My hand on the doorknob, I was about to burst into her room, but stopped myself.

"Crap," I muttered to myself.

This had to be handled delicately. The last thing I wanted to do was hurt her more or make her feel insecure in her own home.

"Payton?" I called through the door. "Honey, open up, please. Let me explain, sweetheart."

Zach glared at me as he stopped forward to knock incessantly on Payton's door. "See what you did? You just had to say that, didn't you?"

He was blaming me for her reaction? My stomach twisted as I worried about Payton and fumed at the same time. And here I honestly thought he was a good guy when I met him. I should have left him in the shower—or better yet, lock his reeking ass out on the front steps until morning.

"Now it's my fault?" I snapped. "You're the one who's unbearable to live with."

"You've only lived with me for a week!"

"Arguing's not going to help," I said through gritted

teeth. *Junk punching him, however, might be of some benefit right now.*

"You don't know how *not* to argue with me, Emma!"

Ignoring him, I knocked again. "Please, Payton?"

"This is ridiculous. Payton, we're coming in." Zach turned the knob and threw open the door.

I hung back, unsure what to do next. Zach just rushed to Payton's side on the edge of the bed and hugged her. The little girl immediately fell into her uncle's embrace, sobbing. They stayed in that position for what seemed like hours until she looked up to me.

"Do you want to leave me too, Emma?" she asked, her voice small and weak.

My heart broke at the sound and her words pulled me towards her like a powerful magnet. I knelt in front of the two of them.

"No, I don't, Pay." I sighed. "There were just some things that your uncle did that upset me."

Understatement of the year.

Zach made some noise beside her and I glared at him over Payton's head. Payton moved from his embrace into my arms. I kissed the top of her head.

"I don't want you to go, Emma."

"I won't leave you," I whispered, my chest tight. "I promise."

Her little chin set, she gave a short nod. "Okay." Apparently, she considered our verbal contract binding. "I'm hungry. Can we have breakfast?"

Boing! The way kids bounced back never failed to disorient me. I let out a laughing sigh. "Sure, honey. French toast?"

She nodded her head, then turned to Zach. "We have to brush our teeth first."

It was a good thing that it was so easy to comfort her. If only it was that easy for me. As the pair of them disappeared down the hall, I remained kneeling on Payton's bedroom floor. My hands rubbed up and down my thighs as my heartbeat returned to a normal rhythm.

This job was turning into more than… a job. My attachment to Payton was growing, and my feelings about her uncle were getting complicated. *What now?*

About ten minutes later, Payton joined me in the kitchen. "Uncle Zach is taking a shower," she informed me as she climbed onto the stool at the breakfast bar.

I didn't comment and instead asked her if she had any nightmares. She often forgot her night terrors, but I certainly didn't. Quietly, she shook her head. We were almost done eating when Zach joined us.

When we were finished and I was washing the dishes, Zach spoke. "Sweets, could you play with your dolls in your room? Emma and I need to talk."

She looked anxious. "Are you two going to fight again?"

Zach and I glanced at each other and then back at her.

"We won't," he promised.

Payton lingered in the kitchen for a moment before obeying her uncle, leaving us in silence. The sound of the water gurgling as it swirled down the sink drain seemed abnormally loud.

I didn't know what to say, and apparently neither did Zach.

If I was being totally honest with myself, his behavior last night not only disgusted me, but disappointed me. I thought he was better than that. I *wanted* him to be better than that. Seeing him like that… well, it hurt me.

"Emma."

"What?"

"What was that earlier?"

I sighed and dried my hands. "I told you, Zach. Payton's my main responsibility in this household, but you coming home drunk makes you mine too."

"I didn't ask you to—"

"And in all honesty," I interrupted him, "you need to *stop* coming home like that. Do you want her to see you in that state? Her parents died because of a drunk driver!"

I knew he took a cab or something when he went out, so I wasn't worried about him on the road. He was stupid, but not unsafe. I was more concerned that his messy, emotional, uncontrolled state might frighten his young niece. Hell, it scared me.

Zach went quiet and leaned against the counter, his arms crossed. "Are you telling me to give up that part of my life because I'm supposed to be a 'parent' to my niece?"

"I'm telling you that you could have that part of your life scheduled. Once a week or twice. But not consecutively," I replied, realizing we had to find a compromise.

"Fine." He sighed. Chances were that our conversation was not over. "But we have to apologize to her first."

"I have a pretty good idea of how we could," I said and the two of us headed over to Payton's room.

She stopped playing the moment we entered, and I

could see the tension rolling off of her. "Are you done talking now?"

For now, thank god, I thought to myself. Chances were that our conversation was not over.

I squatted in front of her and smiled. "What do you say we go to the aquarium today?"

Her eyes widened and she squealed, jumping into my arms. "Really?"

"Absolutely," I replied, kissing the top of her head and then helping her up, "C'mon, let's get ready."

Zach stood in the doorway, leaning against the frame, a faint smile on his face. I raised my eyebrow at him, and he suddenly seemed to snap back into reality. He merely nodded and retreated to his own room, allowing Payton and me to get ready.

～

*B*y the time we were on the road and heading to the aquarium, it was nearly lunchtime. Zach and I rode silently, him driving and me riding shotgun, while Anderson and Payton debated in the back seat over what was the cutest marine animal.

Zach invited Anderson to come with us, or maybe it was an order. In any case, he and Payton had gotten close with all the babysitting he'd been doing with me. I was pretty sure that when Anderson signed his contract to be football star Zach Pennington's personal assistant, he didn't anticipate moving to Denver to play with Barbies.

"C'mon, c'mon, let's go!" Payton said when we arrived, jumping up and down in the parking lot. She grabbed both my and Zach's hands and pulled us with surprising force to the entrance. Anderson followed slowly behind, saying he wanted to make a few phone calls.

"Slow down, Payton," I said gently.

It was like talking to a brick wall. Or her uncle. She was dancing around like she had live snakes in her shorts.

"Come. *On!*"

"We have to get tickets first, sweets," Zach reminded her, throwing his arms around her to stop her from barreling inside. But her enthusiasm was contagious, as was her smile.

The ticket lady grinned at the three of us.

"You have a beautiful kid," she commented as she handed Zach our tickets.

My heart stopped for one infinitesimal moment. Zach and I glanced at each other but were ushered forward by Payton before we could say that we weren't her parents.

Payton dragged us around to see every single exhibit, tank, display, and pool they had there. Then she wanted to see them again. She was so hyped that I couldn't help but laugh. I'd never seen her that happy since I'd known her.

I promise to help you feel like this more often, I said silently to her as I watched her wide-eyed joy over the penguins.

We had a late lunch before catching anything we missed—to which Payton was happy to guide us. She then played a quiz game they had for kids and won, which made Zach insanely proud of her. When the day finally came to an end and the four of us headed home, both she and Anderson were fast asleep in the backseat.

Zach had to carry Payton inside when we arrived,

and she stirred awake when he was about to set her on the bed. I helped her take a bath and she asked if we could tuck her in bed.

"Could you read me a story?"

I handed Zach a book and we sat on opposite edges of Payton's bed as she lay between us. Zach began to read the Dr. Seuss book that I gave him. He closed the book once he finished it and turned to Payton, whose eyes were getting droopier by the second.

"Tuck me in again tomorrow?" she asked quietly.

"It's a date." Zach kissed her forehead. "Goodnight, sweets."

Once we left her room, we both headed to the sofa and sank into its comfort with matching sighs slipping from our mouths. Now that I'd stopped moving, I realized how tired I was.

I turned to Zach. "She had a good day."

"Yeah. I haven't seen her that happy since... well, you know."

I shifted so I was facing him. "I meant what I said, Zach. I know I'm in no position to tell you how you're supposed to live your life, but Payton does really need you. She was hysterical that time before I moved in because she was so scared that you would leave her, too."

"This time, she thought you were leaving," Zach reminded me quietly. "I know that feeling. I felt that anxiety when I was young, too—when my parents died and all I had was Dean. I thought he hated the fact that he was stuck with me."

I was surprised to hear him suddenly opening up. I wanted to tell him that he didn't need to talk about it if he didn't want to but he had this faraway look in his eyes as he began to quietly recount his story to me. "Our mother died first. She had cancer. My dad...he died a year after. He also died in an accident. Almost the same as Dean and Maggie."

"Dean practically raised me. We also lived with our grandparents for a while but when Dean turned eighteen, I went with him. He gave me a house and food and everything I needed. He was at every game I had, taking time off from work if he had to, just to show me that I was loved and supported like every other kid in school."

It was sometimes easy to forget that it wasn't just Payton who was grieving. Zach lost his brother, too—who happened to be who raised him and his only family for close to half his life. My heart suddenly ached for the boy beside me.

"It must be nice growing up with parents," he said, tilting his head at me.

I turned away. "I wouldn't know. My mother died giving birth to me and my Dad died when I was six." You'd think after so many years that the story would be easy to tell but my throat still tightened every time.

Zach blinked and reached to touch my hand. "Who...?"

"Raised me?" I asked, finishing his question for him. "I moved from foster home to foster home until I turned eighteen." I gave him a weak smile. "Like training to be an Olympic couch surfer."

He watched me carefully, his eyes darkening. "Is that why you weren't hesitant to take care of Payton?"

"I know what it's like to grow up without parents to take care of you. It's all I ever wanted as a child," I said quietly, turning away from him again, "I swore to myself that if I was given the chance, I wouldn't let a child feel what I felt."

"Which was why you took on Payton." Zach mused.

And you.

He smiled. "I probably never thanked you properly."

The expression on my face apparently said, *'Nope!'* His smile was almost shy now.

"Thank you for that, Emma. I honestly don't know what I'd do if I hadn't found you."

It was probably the nicest thing he'd ever said to me, and it shouldn't have made the lump in my throat swell —but it did. "Well, we orphans have to stick together."

He chuckled and squeezed my hand. It was only then that I realized he was holding it. He gave me a crooked smile and I was suddenly aware of how close together we were sitting.

There was no denying it—Zach Pennington was a hazard to my equilibrium. Never before had a man affected me like this. One minute I wanted to be wrapped in his arms like Payton, and the next minute I was tempted to smother him with a stuffed toy.

His strong body and gorgeous face made my heart beat faster, but it was all the other parts of him that drew me to him like a magnet. His love for Payton, his commitment to his job, his sense of humor, his backside in a pair of jeans…

But Zach was a player—on the field and off. I had to remind myself of that. Wasn't it only that morning I'd given him an ultimatum about spending more time at home? Knowing that, however, did not stop me from staring at his mouth.

"We should probably go to bed," I whispered. "It's been a long day."

My boss—*boss!*—nodded, but leaned closer instead of getting up.

I sat there, frozen by my own conflicting emotions. I wanted him but I couldn't. I needed him though I shouldn't. Before I knew it, I felt his soft lips on mine.

Oh my god!

Deep inside I knew this would happen, but I told myself I could resist him. The truth was that I didn't really want to.

The kiss was sweet and gentle, as if his lips were merely caressing mine in slow motion.

When he pulled away from me, his eyes were dark as they sought my gaze. He bit his lower lip, then smiled that crooked smile that made my heart swoon.

"Zach…"

"Goodnight, Emma."

ZACH

he smell of food wafting under my door woke me up. I sat up slowly, rubbed the sleep out of my eyes and checked the clock. It was seven in the morning. I usually got up at 6:30, Payton knocking on my door five minutes later carrying my toothbrush.

But not this morning.

Suddenly I felt panicked, worried that something was wrong. It was a feeling that I had frequently since Dean and Maggie died. Was this what parenting was really like—constant anxiety and frustration? Every day, my respect for my brother and his wife deepened. I only wished I'd had the chance to tell them that.

I rushed out of my room. The moment I stepped into the hall, the smell of bacon and eggs intensified. I followed it to the kitchen to find Emma and Payton dancing around and singing at the top of their lungs into spatula microphones.

Okay, maybe anxiety, frustration, and laughter.

As quickly as my fear enveloped me when I woke, it dissipated at the sight of my two girls trying to coordinate dance steps. When I burst out laughing the spell was broken and they immediately stopped.

Emma's eyes widened at the sight of me and she quickly pivoted to face the stove, hiding the rising blush that I had seen.

Payton, on the other hand, squealed when she saw me. She jumped into my arms and hugged me tightly. "You're awake!"

I kissed the side of her head as I carried her to sit at the counter. It was impossible not to smile at the feeling of her clinging to me like a monkey.

My gaze sought out Emma again and the memory of her lips on mine filled my head. She faced the stove, allowing me to leisurely take in the curves of her body and the way she pushed her shoulders back.

"I missed my personal alarm clock," I teased Payton.

Emma turned around to face me. Her cheeks were pink and her expression difficult to decipher. "We thought we'd let you sleep. Yesterday was, um, eventful."

I inhaled sharply as the faint taste of her mouth came back to me. She spun away again and I suddenly realized that she felt awkward for what had happened between us.

"Are you hungry?" Payton asked me, looking up at me with her big brown eyes. "We were going to surprise you with breakfast in bed, but you ruined it by waking up."

I laughed and kissed her forehead. "Sorry, sweets, if I'd known then I would've slept longer."

Payton's eyebrows furrowed. "But if you knew then it wouldn't be a surprise!"

Emma laughed, her back still to us. As nice as this view was, I suddenly craved a sight of her smile.

"Good morning, Emma," I said. *Turn around. Come on, turn around.*

"Morning." Her attention remained on the bacon she was frying and the eggs she was cooking.

I tried to get her attention, but she continued to avoid me.

Payton and I were setting the table for the three of us when my phone rang. I stepped out of the kitchen to answer it, since the girls were chattering about getting haircuts. When I returned, my niece looked up at me expectantly from the table, breakfast in front of her.

"Who waffat?" she asked.

I chuckled at the sight of her. *Oh wait, I have to be a dad not just the fun uncle.* "Don't speak with your mouth full," I told her, trying to channel my sister-in-law.

"Sowwy," she said around a mouthful of eggs.

Teaching her good manners was definitely going to be a work in progress. Then again, so were mine. "Well, I guess training is canceled today."

Payton's eyes glimmered with delight as she purposefully swallowed before speaking. "Does that mean we can go to the park today?"

I looked to Emma. "Uh…"

She just sat there, looking amused.

Was this a test? What was the correct answer, here? Both of us wanted Payton to feel loved, even if it was different from the relationship she had with Dean and Maggie. That didn't mean, however, saying 'yes' to everything she asked for. Right?

This parenting thing was hard. Some days I wasn't sure if I was up to it. Okay, most days. Emma was definitely better at it than I was. The conversation she and I had the night before, about her ending up in a series of foster homes, suddenly came back to me.

God, was it actually possible that Payton could have been in the same situation? If I hadn't taken her, then… well, yeah. How fucked up was that? How could I have contemplated the alternative, even for a second?

I looked at my niece and smiled, nodding my head slowly. She just about levitated off her chair.

"Can we go now?"

"Sure. But don't you have a class or something?" I asked as I tried in vain to remember her schedule.

Since it was June, the school year was done. She'd just finished kindergarten, I think. Maggie had pre-registered her in a zillion activities over the summer. After I arrived in Denver for good, I'd thought about cancelling them, until Emma reminded me that keeping Payton busy meant she slept better at night. Emma and Anderson were always the ones who moved her back and forth, though, while I adjusted to the new team and environment.

"Oh! You can come with us!"

Payton sounded so excited and I knew that I couldn't refuse. Her heart had been broken a couple of times recently; how much more heartbreak could a little girl take?

Apparently, parenting was basically about trying to avoid feeling guilty.

"Sure, sweets, what do you have today?"

Emma answered for her. "It's Monday, so I guess dance."

"Okay." I could watch little girls in tutus.

"And piano," she added, "and art in the afternoon."

Wow. This kid better be a fucking prodigy at something. I didn't even know we had a piano.

"And we better get ready, sweetheart," Emma said as she put her plate in the sink.

Once we were done with our breakfast, showers, and getting dressed, I grabbed the keys to my car. "Let's go!"

Emma put her hand on my shoulder. "Um, your car isn't child-friendly, Zach."

I stared at the Challenger sitting peacefully in the garage and then at Emma. "Then how are we driving her to her lessons?"

Just as I spoke, Anderson rolled up in a minivan. I hadn't called him, so either Emma had or he was just used to the schedule. He got out of the van and looked at me with surprise. "No training today?"

I rolled my eyes, knowing full well that he always knew my schedule before I did. I turned to Emma. "You're not gonna make me drive that thing." It was a *minivan.*

"Oh, yeah," Emma said with a grin on her face.

She chuckled and opened the door for Payton, who jumped into a booster seat. Anderson tossed me the keys before sliding into the backseat with Payton.

I grudgingly got in the driver's seat and whined, "You didn't complain about my car yesterday."

"That's why I'm complaining now. We were cooped up in that car yesterday. More leg space here. Not to mention that you didn't have a booster seat for Payton," Emma pointed out.

I huffed and said no more until we'd deposited Payton at dance.

"So, what do you do while she's in class?" I asked

Emma outside, leaning against the stupid minivan that basically ripped away my masculinity.

Anderson didn't even look up from his phone. "We can go for coffee while we wait," he said. "I have to get your schedule fixed for next month. You've been getting calls from companies for endorsements."

I smirked. "Oh, the price of being this handsome and talented."

Emma made a scoffing sound deep in her throat and headed off to the café without even a glance backward at the two of us. Quickly Anderson fell into step beside her.

I watched as the two of them chatted, suddenly feeling out of place.

At the coffee shop I cleared my throat behind them as they ordered, and the all-knowing Anderson ordered for me. The three of us took our seats and I fidgeted with my phone as my assistant alternated phone calls with conversations with Emma.

I wanted to talk to her, but every time I tried to she just gave me one-word answers or shut me down completely.

In the car afterwards, Payton asked if we could have lunch at the park. So, while she had art lessons, the three of us bought lunch and a blanket to spread out at the park for a picnic. Before Payton was done, Emma received a call from her piano teacher that today's lesson was cancelled. Payton was thrilled because it meant she could play longer at the park.

I couldn't remember the last time I'd been with my niece like this, just making up silly games and being together.

I didn't even check my phone.

We played on the monkey bars, the swings then the slides, and I found my heart filling more and more each time I heard Payton's infectious laughter. We were playing tag with Emma and Anderson when she spotted a classmate from dance class. With our permission she went to play with her, and we three adults headed back to the blanket.

"She has so much energy." Emma admired Payton from our position under the trees.

"No kidding." I was exhausted. "She could run drills sometime for us, give the coaches the day off."

Anderson laughed, knowing that I wasn't totally joking.

"Uncle Zach!"

I turned my attention to my niece. "Yes?"

She and her friend rushed up to us. "Can I have a sleepover at Ethan's? Pleeeaaaase! You can pick me up tomorrow at their house. Emma and Andy know where it is."

I turned to Emma who smiled at Payton and then nodded at me. "They have play dates sometimes."

"I have to ask Ethan's mom…"

Right on cue, a blonde woman appeared beside Ethan. I looked at her and she smiled warmly at us. "Payton already asked me. I'm fine with it. They have play dates and sleepovers all the time…"

Her voice trailed off and I knew that she meant to say that she and Maggie would arrange play dates for the kids.

I found myself nodding. "Well, if you're okay with it then I guess I am, too."

Ethan and Payton squealed with delight and started chasing each other around the picnic blanket.

"I'm Serena, by the way." She stuck out her hand.

"Zach. And that's Anderson and Emma."

Serena nodded. "I know. I've met them before, but it's finally nice to get the chance to meet Payton's uncle. She talks highly of you and my husband loved you even when you ruined Denver's streak."

At least someone in Denver liked me. "That's nice to hear."

Serena simply smiled. "Well, you guys can go while I round those two up. You can have Anderson bring me her clothes if you want. He knows the address."

Just how much of Payton's life had I been missing out on?

"Yeah, sure," said Anderson. "C'mon, Zach, we should head home."

Payton hugged me and kissed me on the cheek and did the same thing to Emma and Anderson. Then the three of us headed home and Emma packed a bag for Anderson to take to Serena's house. Before I knew it, he was out the door again.

Emma and I were alone for the first time all day.

Finally.

ZACH

I followed Emma into the kitchen, where she looked in the fridge.

"I'm ordering pizza," I announced.

She threw me a relieved smile. "Great."

My forehead furrowed as I pulled up the app on my phone. I wondered if she didn't really like cooking but did it because it had become part of her job. She was so good at it, though. What else did she do for us, just because she was the nanny?

After I placed the order, I found Emma in the living room. I blinked at the sight of her sitting cross-legged on the velvety sofa with a bright pink cushion over her lap like a shield. Suddenly it occurred to me that furniture with throw pillows was essentially the adult equivalent of Payton's bed full of stuffed animals.

It still gave me a start every time I realized this was my home now. Maggie went for a bohemian kind of style that didn't really suit me, but I didn't have the heart to change anything. Well, maybe the floofy curtains could go, and about twenty damn pillows. I'd chucked six of them into the guest bedroom closet when I arrived.

As if she'd read my mind, Emma tilted her head. "Do you miss Florida?"

I shrugged. "I lived there because I played there."

"What about your friends?"

"Well, I—" I stopped. *Huh.* "I didn't really have a lot," I realized out loud.

"Really?"

"I'd go out with teammates." Clubbing and blowing off steam, mostly, but I didn't think Emma would want to hear about picking up jersey chasers. "But mostly all I did was work. Train, play, travel."

"And your brother was here. Was it hard to be away from your only family?"

I blinked.

"I'm sorry." She looked down at her lap. "That was kind of nosy. I was just curious."

"It's okay." And it was. I was just as interested in her. I wanted to know what her favorite food was, what she dreamed about as a teenager, what kind of panties she wore.

The conversation was put on hold as the pizza arrived. We fell upon the open box in comfortable silence, and I thought about what Emma had asked.

"Dean and Maggie wanted to raise Payton like a normal kid," I said after my first piece. "Not around a bunch of celebrity bullshit."

They'd been so proud of me when I was drafted, and even more so as my talent made me a household name. That was the problem, though. I was busy with endorsements, sponsors, flying around the country, and in the weight room or on the field the rest of the time. I barely had time for Netflix, much less spending a lot of time with Payton.

"Were you close to Payton before?" she asked, halfway through her second piece. "I mean, I know you're her favorite uncle and all."

I snorted. "*Only* uncle." Maggie had been an only child. Damn, I kept forgetting to get Payton on Skype with her grandparents in New Zealand.

"Did you visit much?"

"When I could, mostly at holidays." *Except when we played on Christmas. Or Thanksgiving.* I frowned, feeling regretful and grumpy.

Emma began to round up our plates and I helped her. I hadn't realized that we had finished half of the box. I dried the dishes as she washed them and then we both moved to the living room with our wine glasses refilled and sitting close together on the couch.

"My turn for questions."

"Okay," she said apprehensively.

"Why'd you have to be stuck in foster care? You didn't have *any* other family?"

She swallowed a big gulp of wine before answering. "Not really. My mom and dad actually came here from Ireland, basically eloping."

"Romantic."

"More like impulsive and rebellious." Her smile faded. "They were different religions, and their parents didn't like that so much. Then I came along and my mother died…"

"Right. I'm sorry."

She shrugged. "I think they blamed my dad. And my father's side couldn't forgive him running off." Her chuckle had a hard edge to it. "Family drama."

"Didn't you miss having more family?"

"Hard to miss what you never had."

I got the feeling that Emma felt the loss more than she let on. I couldn't resist reaching out to squeeze her arm. "If it counts, Payton and I could be your family."

She looked down, blushing. "Thanks."

I put down my wine before cradling her chin and lifting her face to meet my gaze. "Hey, they're the ones who missed out."

"That's sweet."

Didn't she get it? "Emma, I lost my parents. Now my brother and the closest thing I had to a sister. But I never realized how lucky I was in my life until I met you."

"Wow." With a trembling hand, she set her glass down beside mine on the coffee table. "That's a hell of a line."

I shook my head. "I've honestly never said anything like that in my life."

Emma looked at me and sighed. "Look, Zach, about last night…"

I dragged my thumb over her lips to hold in any regrets she had. "I was the one who kissed you. That's on me, and you know what? I'm not apologizing and I'm not taking it back. All I want is to have the chance to kiss you again." *Lots.*

Emma's eyes widened. "Oh."

I leaned in, as though in slow motion, and replaced my thumb with my lips.

As my mouth slanted to cover hers, she gave a hitching little sigh of submission and melted into me.

Yes!

I pulled her tight against me, but she still wasn't close enough. Her lips parted, her tongue tentatively touching mine. With a growl of satisfaction, I intensified the kiss until we were forced to draw back enough to catch our breath—but not for long.

Our lips collided again and this time, it felt different. I was more aggressive this time around, kissing her with the passion that had built up inside of me all day as I spent it with her.

I'd known beautiful women, but they were all too aware of their looks. It was all surface stuff, I now realized. Everything in my life had been superficial until now. Other than Dean and Maggie, I didn't allow anyone close enough to share my triumphs or fears.

Until Emma.

Emma's beauty and spirit shone from inside her. Whether she was sipping coffee or tucking Payton into bed, her every movement was graced with elegance and warmth. She couldn't possibly know how lovely she was.

I needed to show her.

Her hands flew to my neck as mine slipped under her shirt. She gasped at the feel of my palms sweeping up her ribs.

"Wait," she whispered, pulling away.

I groaned but stopped. My body felt overheated, straining with desire, but I let her hold me at arms' length. I searched her gaze, licking my lips.

Damn, had I crossed a line? Had I pushed too far?

Emma's eyes burned bright and before I knew it, she crashed her lips into mine and tugged at my shirt. My hands resumed their rightful place against her skin.

"Please, Zach." Her voice was breathless. "I want you. All of you."

I'd already begun to open my soul up to her. Worshipping her body would be like running on the field—like I was born to do it. She wanted me? Well, then I would give her everything I had in me, and I would take anything she offered of herself.

From that point on, there was no hesitation. No more shyness. We came together with equal force.

I carried her to my bedroom and threw her gently on the unmade bed, removing my clothes before our lips met again. Soon enough, her clothes joined mine on the floor and we were tangled together on the bed.

Instinct led us. Passion overcame us.

I kissed every part of her body and every inch of skin I could put my mouth on, wandering over her like a blind man memorizing her. She writhed beneath me, moaning my name over and over again. By the time I sank myself inside of her, her sighs and screams were more than primal responses of pleasure and need.

They made my heart happy.

EMMA

*T*he sunlight woke me up. In the back of my mind, I automatically listened for Payton stirring but heard nothing. Looked like I had a few lazy moments to myself. Yay! I smiled to myself, my eyes still closed against the day as I stretched.

And hit something warm and firm at my side.

Uh oh.

I let out a gasp, my eyes popping open to find Zach sleeping beside me.

Naked.

As was I.

While my brain struggled to process everything, my body went into fight or flight mode. I clutched the sheet to me and rolled away from him like he was a grenade about to go off.

You know how in movies, when this kind of thing happens, the heroine always lands with a gentle thud with a sheet draped elegantly around her?

Well... With a very naked, heavy, naked Zach Pennington sleeping on top of the other end of the sheet, I'd rolled myself into the sheet and now dangled off the side of the bed like a weird cocoon.

"Fuff!"

My face was smushed against the side of the mattress, my arms bound over my breasts. For some reason, gravity was not working for me. I was stuck. I wriggled a little, trying to free myself.

Nope.

This was ridiculous, and I was starting to sweat. I'd seen newborns break out of swaddling more easily than this. Maybe there was a way to jiggle the bed, so I'd be shaken loose like a recalcitrant candy bar perched in a vending machine that just ate your money.

"Mofferfuff."

Yeah, you try to move a queen size mattress with your forehead and get back to me.

I panted with frustration, my breath hot and damp against my own face. The sound of Zach's heavy, even breathing told me that he was clueless to my predicament, thankfully.

Finally, I freed an arm and flung it over the top of the bed. With the sheet clenched in my fist, I tugged *hard* and landed with a loud thump on the floor. Wincing, I lay there silently and took stock of my injuries.

Okay, I was hiding.

It was a good thing that Zach slept soundly. *Very* soundly. Actually, if I hadn't heard his low snores, I would have been tempted to put a mirror up to his face to make sure he was still alive. I just could imagine it now on ESPN:

"Breaking news! Star football player Zach Pennington's tenure in Denver was cut short today—not by a contract dispute, but by his young niece's nanny. Poor judgment and amazing sex are suspected to be involved."

Speaking of, as I stood up my body twinged in ways that had nothing to do with falling off the bed. I crept out of the room with the sheet loosely wrapped around me. It wasn't until I got into the hallway and closed his bedroom door behind me, that I remembered Payton was at Serena's house.

Thank god. The last thing I needed right now was an interrogation from my charge about why I was wearing Uncle Zach's bedding. For one thing, I would be mortified. Secondly, I didn't have any age-appropriate answers.

I sank onto the sofa, the memories of last night flashing through my mind as fast as a moving train. Squeezing my eyes shut, I rubbed my palm against my forehead. Disbelief coursed through me. What...? How...?

Did I seriously just have sex with my boss?

I felt so stupid. The only thing than being worse than a walking cliché is being a horizontal one.

My gaze fell upon the wine glasses on the table, but I knew they weren't to blame. I needed time to think about what to do next. I decided to pick up Payton at Serena's. Call me a chicken, but there was no way in hell that I was ready to do a post-mortem on the night before.

I dropped the sheet in the laundry basket by the mudroom, uncomfortably aware that I was walking around someone else's house totally naked. As I was pulling clothes out, I realized that I might smell... different to Payton. It had been my experience that little kids and animals tended to prefer the natural odor a person carried, not perfumes and lotions—or the musky scent of Zach's body pressed against mine.

Dear god, what have I managed to get myself into?

My face burned at the memories of our passionate encounter fresh in my mind. I stood in the living room, my arms wrapped around me as I recalled where his tongue had gone and unguarded words that we'd said to each other. Part of me didn't want to wash him off of me, to keep his primal stamp of ownership.

A bigger part of me decided to risk taking the extra time for the most efficient shower in history.

The moment the water hit my overheated body, I sucked in a deep breath. Right, it was time to face reality, even if I wasn't ready to face my currently naked employer. I needed to be a mature, rational adult and not slam my head against the tile. As I skimmed my body with a soapy poof, I imagined his touch.

His mouth.

His…

Okay, shower time was over.

I dressed at record speed, grateful that Zach hadn't woken up in the meantime. Remember? *Bock bock bock.* But I would use the time walking over to Ethan's house to clear my head.

Under the bright blue sky, I tried to think rationally about this. In my defense, we made no promises to each other. We were grown-ups and both consented. And it wasn't as though he'd taken my virginity, nor did I feel compelled to write "Mrs. Emma Pennington" on my Math binder over and over again.

Been there, done that, got the souvenir heartbreak.

My only other intimate experience was with a guy

that I thought was special and loyal. Unfortunately, he just thought I was easy pickings.

Once people found out I'd been a foster kid, their perception of me would suddenly change. They wondered if I'd lived in some kind of twisted melo-drama, like a VC Andrews novel. Then, like my first and only boyfriend, they figured I was so desperate for affec-tion and attention that I would do anything for it.

Was that what Zach thought of me?

"Emma!"

I jumped slightly at the sound of Serena's voice, surprised I'd already arrived. A million thoughts preoc-cupied me all the way there. Frankly, I was lucky I hadn't been hit by a car.

"Hi, Serena." I smiled at her. Serena was a lovely woman, the kind I never met when I lived in my tiny apartment in a sketch neighborhood. Even the people who fostered me weren't as nice as Serena and Bryan. "How was Payton last night?"

"Such a doll to be with," Serena replied. "They're having breakfast with Bryan. Come inside."

Something kept my feet glued to the walkway, until the front door suddenly flew open and Payton bounded out of the house. My heart swelled with the sigh of her as she rushed to meet me. I barely managed to catch her, stumbling back a little as she jumped on me.

"Emma! I missed you!" She hugged me tightly, then tilted her head back to grin at me.

My eyes widened. "Did you lose another tooth?" And I missed it. *Rats*.

Payton nodded, then whispered conspiratorially to me, "But I put it in a tissue in my pocket. I didn't want the Tooth Fairy to get confused last night and give

Ethan money. Can we put it under my pillow when we get home?"

Heart. Melt. "Of course, honey." It was official—Payton was probably the sweetest girl I've ever met my entire life. I kissed the side of her head and hefted her securely in my arms. "Were you good for Miss Serena?"

She frowned. "Of course!"

I chuckled and hugged her tightly for a moment. Like a kitten, she soon squirmed in my grasp and I put her down just in time for Ethan to come out of the house.

Serena called out, "Slow down, you two!" as they raced around to the back yard to do heaven knows what.

"They really are best of friends," I commented, shaking my head. Payton was a lucky girl to have people like these to spend time with.

"They were born a month apart. They've known each other since they were babies."

"Ah."

"I guess I never told you that I worked with Maggie before," Serena said.

"No, I didn't know that."

I knew very little about Dean and Maggie, other than what Zach had shared with me and what Payton had told me about them. She focused on the important stuff, such as Dean's ability to burp on command and the cinnamon toast that Maggie made for her.

I'd seen enough pictures of them to know what they looked like. Maggie had been tall with long chestnut hair and a warm smile that Payton inherited. In the family photos around the house Dean looked a lot like Zach, only stockier and shorter. Payton got his eyes, long-lashed brown ones that shone like melted chocolate.

"What were they like?" I asked. "Zach doesn't talk about their personalities, so much. And Payton's memories are... like moments in time."

Serena looked into the distance, a small smile on her face. "Maggie was a brilliant baker. Ethan loved having sleepovers over there because that he got to help Maggie bake." She focused on me again, her smile broadening. "Frankly, I think they just snuck a lot of cookie dough."

It was easy to picture a mischievous Payton and Ethan "helping" Maggie out in the kitchen.

"I miss her," Serena said simply.

"I'm sure."

She tilted her head at me. "For what it's worth, I think you two would've gotten along really well."

That touched me. "I really wish I had the chance to meet them." Though I couldn't see how that would have happened, had they lived. And I never would have met Payton... or Zach. My eyes prickled at the thought.

"Payton has a lot of Dean in her," Serena went on. "They're both stubborn but generous spirit, you know?

I nodded. That definitely sounded like a family trait.

"But Dean was always ready to help people. He coached Payton's soccer team last season because they couldn't find a coach to replace the old one and Payton really wanted to play the game. He didn't want her to lose the opportunity."

It made me sad to think that, now, all future opportunities would be missed. "I wish that they had longer with Payton." *Like, forever*.

"They adored her," Serena agreed, "but Payton says that you and Zach are doing okay."

I blinked. "Payton told you about us? I mean, not that there's an *us*—" I tripped over my own tongue as heat rose in my cheeks. "But, um, helping Payton together?"

"That you and Zach aren't agreeing much on anything and that you two argue?" She chuckled, nodding. "Yeah. She did. She told to me that it bothers her, but she says it's better than the first few days when you two barely talked to each other."

I bit my lip and hung my head low, ashamed. All I wanted was to create a good environment for Payton, but I suddenly felt like arguing with Zach most of the time did more harm to her than good. It also stung a little that Payton didn't feel as though she could come to me or Zach with her concerns.

"I—I—"

Serena raised a hand and smiled at me. "You don't need to explain yourself. Maggie told me about Zach and what he's like. I'd never met him until yesterday, though. He didn't visit that much. I'm sure you just want him to step up and be a father to Payton."

"I don't want him to replace her own father," I said.

"Of course not. Nobody could replace Dean. But Zach's relationship with Payton is obviously going to change now. It kind of has to, if you want her to feel secure and all that."

I smiled gratefully at Serena. "Yes, that's exactly it."

"Then I guess you better make it clear to him," Serena said, her eyes shining. "You know, yesterday was the first time I met him. He's, um…" She reflexively looked around us for little ears. Or maybe her husband. "Hot as fuck."

Now I blushed so hard I was probably radiating heat. "I know, right?"

She winked. "If it wouldn't make things way more complicated and awkward, I'd say go for it."

All I could do was stare at Serena. I didn't even see Payton rush up to me until her head barreled into my belly.

"Emma! Could we get hot chocolate at Tate's?"

"I thought you had breakfast?" I asked, eyeing her. I'd learned the hard way not to give her too many sweets, especially in the mornings.

Serena patted me on the shoulder. "I made spinach omelets for breakfast so you're free from the sugar high for the time being."

"Awesome, thank you! Then I guess we're going to Tate's," I said and then pushed Payton gently towards Serena and Ethan. "Say thank you and goodbye, Pay."

She gave Serena a quick hug before popping back inside to say goodbye to Ethan and his dad. Then she had to rush inside again to grab her overnight bag, which I carried.

It was a good thing that she didn't mind walking all the way to Tate's, which was a dozen blocks from the house. I laughed as she bounded around me on the sidewalk like an excited puppy. The whole way, Payton chattered about what she and her friend had done together.

"Did you, you know, *sleep* at your sleepover?" I teased her.

"Of course, we did. Ethan has a bunkbed!"

I tried to listen attentively as she told me all about being on the top bunk but, all the while, my mind kept replaying my own sleepover with Zach. Like the way I was on the, uh, 'top bunk' with his hands greedily roaming over my body as I writhed on him. When she mentioned the safety rail, I rocked to a halt.

"Emma?"

My heart thudded in my chest as I tried to remember. Yes, we used protection. I was on the Pill regardless, but... yes, I was nearly one hundred percent sure that we used condoms—plural. Ninety percent sure.

Ugh! How freaking awkward would it be to ask him? Maybe I could just check the trash can in the bathroom?

Payton tugged on my hand. "Emma, we're still going, aren't we?"

"Yeah." I shook my head. "Sorry, honey."

When we got to Tate's I ordered Payton hot chocolate and oatmeal cookies, which I found out was her favorite kind. We sat at a little café table outside, where birds waited patiently for me to drop crumbs from my muffin.

Still avoiding Zach, I texted Anderson to ask if he could pick us up and drive us to Payton's piano lesson. She had a piano in the morning and soccer at two in the afternoon, which meant she could have a nap in between. Maybe I would, too.

Suddenly Payton stopped talking and squealed with delight. She jumped out of her seat like a jack-in-the-box and ran off. I immediately turned around to call her back, only to see her jump into Zach's arms.

EMMA

I froze in my seat, my mouth full of muffin.

Zach, being Zach, caught the attention of everyone he passed as he followed Payton to our table—but his gaze was laser sharp on me. When he raised an eyebrow at me, I had to remind myself to swallow. The muffin felt like a block of cement going down. I reached for my coffee, partly just to do something with my hands.

"Didn't know we were going out for breakfast," Zach commented as he dropped into a chair. His tone was both casual and accusatory at the same time. Or maybe that's just how I interpreted it.

Payton wriggled into the seat between us. I was amused to see her pick up her drink and hold it the same way I held mine.

Zach noticed, too.

"Aren't you a bit young for coffee?" he asked, his lips quirking.

Payton looked into her half-full cup. "It's hot chocolate."

He laughed at her. "It's summer. Who drinks hot chocolate in summer?"

"Payton does," I said pointedly as I saw her face fall at the implied criticism from Uncle Zach. I glared at him, and thankfully he got the message.

"Actually, that's really smart," he added. "It stays hot longer, right?"

Payton nodded, perking up again.

Now he turned to me and I could see the questions in his eyes—questions I didn't want to answer and didn't *know how* to answer. "Em—"

I cut him off. "How did you know we were here?"

"Got a text from Anderson. What are you two doing here?"

"I thought it'd be nice to take a walk to get Payton from Serena's."

"Hmmm," Zach mused as he turned his attention to his niece, asking her how she was and if she had fun at Ethan's. I listened to them talk but I caught Zach glancing at me from time to time.

"You want something to eat?" I asked, eager for an opportunity to get away for a few minutes. I went to order him a bacon and egg breakfast sandwich and some coffee.

Although I was hoping to get a moment to myself to think, all I could actually think about was the way I felt Zach's gaze burning on me as I walked away from the table. When I got back, he gave me a grateful smile as he continued to listen intently to his niece.

For only staying one night at a friend's house Payton had an awful lot of adventures to tell Zach about. It suddenly occurred to me that it was probably the first sleepover she'd had since the accident. My heart lurched a little. Had she woken in the night and wanted her mom? Had she missed me and Zach?

"What, Emma?"

"Huh?" I frowned in confusion, until I looked down and discovered that I'd placed my palm high on Payton's back. My thumb rubbed back and forth, unconsciously soothing her. I hadn't even been aware of doing it. I stilled my hand but left it in place.

"Is something wrong?" Zach's forehead creased with worry.

I gave them both what I hoped was a casual, reassuring smile. "No, it's nothing. Finish your story, honey."

As she told Zach about the stairs to the top bunk, I stared at my arm as though it were disconnected from my body. This little girl had gotten so deep into my heart that the desire to comfort her had become a reflex. It was like my soul had reached out for Payton, knowing that we needed each other.

It was time to be honest with myself.

I'd never had another job like this. Never cared for another child this way. Maybe it was the circumstances that were extraordinary or maybe it was just Payton herself, but I found myself longing to be her mother. When I was talking to Serena earlier that morning, I was even a little envious of Maggie for the five years she had with Payton. How screwed up was that?

I was so lost in my thoughts that I followed Zach and Payton to the car without comment. My silence went unnoticed as Zach drove us to piano class. Or, I thought it did.

"Emma, what's going on?" Zach cornered me after Payton had gone into her piano teacher's house.

"What do you mean?"

"You haven't said more than a dozen words since I met up with you two."

I laughed weakly. "It's hard to get in a word edge-wise, with Payton around."

He didn't buy it. "You're mad at me," he decided.

"No, I'm not." My response was automatic, but then I realized I didn't know what I felt. I was confused. Afraid of being hurt. "I'm just…" I waved my hand around. "I don't know."

His eyes narrowed at me, but the expression on his face softened. "Okay. I get it. You need some time. We can talk later."

I nodded.

For the next few hours I remained quiet, while Zach gave me space and focused on Payton—so much so that Anderson met us at soccer and offered to take me home early.

"Why?" I asked him.

"Zach thought you needed a break. He's got this," he said, motioning to his employer and Payton doing a drill together.

The sight of the handsome professional athlete and the adorable little girl kicking the ball back and forth garnered the attention of more than a few of the moms. I couldn't blame them, but I still felt a compulsion to do something to mark Zach and Payton as mine.

What the hell was wrong with me?

"Well?" Anderson waved his car key in front of me.

I turned to the field and called Zach's name. He said something to Payton and jogged over to me and Anderson.

"You okay if I go home?" I was suddenly feeling drained.

"Of course. We're fine."

They really were. Zach was stepping up, just the way I'd asked him to. Before I could say anything more, Zach kissed me on the cheek and sprinted back onto the field. Nearby, I heard an appreciative hum.

"I'll see you at home later!" I yelled. It was possessive, irrational and childish of me, but I still felt satisfied when I saw the envious looks of the drooling soccer moms on the sidelines. *Yeah, they're mine, bitches.*

The rest of the day went by quickly. I indulged in a nap on Payton's bed when I got home and woke up to find Zach and Payton inhaling plates of spaghetti in the dining room. All too soon, it was bath time and bed for Payton, who was crashing hard. After Zach had closed his niece's bedroom door, he sat down beside me on the couch.

"You ready to talk now?"

I'd already decided that there was a lot I needed to keep to myself. The chances of me getting hurt were too high. "About what?"

He gave me a disbelieving look. "Last night."

"Oh. It was the wine."

"No, it wasn't. It was you and me. Maybe it was inevitable, but I'm not going to take it back and don't ask me to forget it. And then you ghosted on me this morning!"

"I was trying to save us both the awkward morning after." Except now it was the awkward evening after.

"You're the only one who felt that way, Emma!" Zach said, exasperation seeping into his tone.

I ground my teeth in irritation and I popped up from the couch. "Maybe *I* want to take it back," I said, trying to keep my voice steady as I paced. "I'm not one of your conquests nor the girls that throw themselves at you."

He looked like I'd punched him. "Did I treat you like one?"

I stopped. Shook my head. No, of course he hadn't.

It was special.

It was hot.

It was revelatory.

"It was a mistake, that's all."

His expression was thunderous as he stood and strode toward me. "Bullshit. It was fucking amazing." He took another step closer to me and tilted my face up, forcing me to look at him. "And you know it."

It's really hard to argue with someone who's right.

"Zach, I can't…" I sagged a little as he cradled my face with both his hands.

"Can't what, baby?"

I didn't know what to say. He was too close, his breath hot on my face.

"Tell me, Emma, don't you want me?" His voice was low and rough, but I heard the insecurity hiding there— like Payton afraid that I was going to leave.

I couldn't move, paralyzed by his gaze, his question echoing in the recesses of my brain. My heart pounded in my chest, my blood racing through my body so swiftly I wondered how he didn't feel my pulse throbbing at my jaw.

I wanted him.

I knew it in my heart, deep down, but was afraid to admit it even to myself. It was like loving Payton. I couldn't help it, but chances were that I was going to get hurt in the end. I had to protect myself, didn't I?

"I can't," I said.

He tilted his head at me, his mouth curving in a tight smile. "That's not the same as you don't."

"Then I *don't*."

"Liar," he growled.

Like a flash of lightning, his hands dropped from my face and down my body. He picked me up and pressed me against the wall that I'd instinctively backed into. My legs locked around his waist as his mouth fell on mine.

His kiss was possessive and passionate. I could taste the frustration he felt towards me earlier and his aggression showed in his kiss. Last night he'd been gentler. Now he stripped away my defenses, demanding my honesty.

I kissed him back.

"Say you want me," he whispered against my lips.

"I do, damn you."

He carried me to his room and tossed me on the bed, locking the door before rushing to me again. Our clothes were off in a matter of seconds, thrown to the floor without a second thought.

Any second thoughts I might have had also hit the floor, as his kiss turned from an attack to a seduction. He bent over me, his mouth tracing a path down my neck to my breasts. A gasp escaped me as he sucked my nipple into his mouth.

"Say it, Emma. I need you to say it."

His hot breath washed over me like an invisible brand, the sensation of his skin against mine making me shiver. Something let loose in me. My greed matched his, my hands exploring every inch of his skin I could reach.

"I want you, I want you, I want you."

When he raised his head to meet my gaze his eyes

were dark and wild with lust, but the grin on his face was pure Zach. "Told you so."

"You arrogant bastard," I hissed, my back arching as his mouth dropped to my other breast.

"Maybe so," he murmured, "but I need you more than anything else in the world right now." I let out a little yelp as he bit gently on my nipple, then released it. He looked me in the eye again. "If I act arrogant, it's only because *I have you*."

Then he lowered his head, his gaze and hands roaming over me with reverence.

He kissed a path down my body, circling my navel with his tongue. Then he lay between my legs, his large hands spreading my thighs open. I inhaled sharply when he sucked my clit into his mouth, then sighed as he teased me with little flicks of his tongue. When he nipped at me, I twitched with jolts of delight.

"Oh god, more," I begged him. My hands went to his head, my fingers stroking through his hair.

Without abandon, he began dragging his tongue over me with long, wet, relentless strokes. My moans rose in pitch and volume with each pass of his greedy mouth, until he clapped a hand over my mouth to remind me that we weren't alone.

It was a shock to remember that we weren't the only people in the universe, much less the house. In the back of my head I wondered how it so quickly came to this, why I was back on the bed I had left that morning, and how our conversation wasn't even finished.

But I wanted this just as much as he did and if I didn't, I could've told him to stop and I knew that he would. Instead, I prayed this would never end.

I wanted him to rise over me and fill me, own me

with his cock, stretch me until I didn't know I ended and he began.

I wanted his groans echoing in my ears, along with the creaks of the bed as he pounded into me.

If there was one thing that crossed my mind before I allowed myself to succumb to the blinding pleasure, it was the fact that I had truly crossed the line between an employer and an employee.

The problem was, I couldn't honestly care less at the moment.

ZACH

I'd heard it said that time flies by when you're enjoying your life. In my case, time seemed to be wearing a booster pack because I honestly didn't know where the days—the *weeks*—went.

Since Emma and I compromised on how we took care of Payton, each day was easier than the day before. I never thought I'd love my niece more than I already did but as we learned more about each other I wondered if there was a limit to that love. Now I understood a little of what Dean and Maggie felt. I used to tease my brother about how much he gushed about his daughter but now I did the same thing.

Work had been easier, too. Coach didn't give me that much hell anymore and my teammates had begun warming up to me. Again, it was due to Payton. She, Emma and Anderson paid me a surprise visit one day and she somehow got two dozen professional athletes playing "Red Light, Green Light." Almost instantly, everyone fell in love with her. Even Coach was bugging me about when she could come "help" with training again.

If the days felt like they were speeding by then the nights with Emma felt endless.

I was more than a little embarrassed to admit that I actually liked spending my evenings watching movies or playing board games with Payton and Emma. Instead of trying to duck out to a club or something, I preferred to tuck Payton in and watch her fall asleep as I read to her.

I know—cue the vomit, right? I wouldn't have been surprised to find birds chirping around my head and squirrels dancing at my fucking feet like I was living in a Disney movie.

After Payton was asleep and I led Emma to our bedroom, though, there was nothing G-rated about what happened next.

I honestly didn't imagine that I would like the life I'd end up living in Denver. I'd enjoyed the fast-paced, party scene and bachelor life that Florida offered me. At first, I hated how I had been handed the responsibility to raise Payton but now, I wouldn't trade it for the world. I still grieved my brother and Maggie, but now I'm grateful that Dean listed me as Payton's guardian.

Because if I was asked to name one good thing about my life right now, Payton would be the answer.

And Emma.

"What's with the dopey smile on your face?" Emma asked, snuggling closer to me. "And how are you awake before me?"

Chuckling, I glanced at the clock. It was five in the morning. Somehow Emma always managed to wake up at that time without having an alarm clock. I drew circles on her bare shoulder and kissed the top of her head.

"I woke up at around four and couldn't go back to sleep," I said.

She kissed my shoulder and then propped her head up with her arm. Her dark hair cascaded down her shoulders in wavy locks, her blue eyes bright and her lips swollen and enticing. I leaned close and kissed her.

It was another twenty minutes before I let her out of bed. Emma smiled back at me as she stood up and searched for her clothes. I sat up in bed, admiring the view.

"Were you going to get Payton's school supplies today?" I asked her.

Emma nodded as she slipped on her panties. "Yep. You want to come?"

"Sure."

When she pulled on my shirt, which fell to her thighs, my body tightened. I reached over and tugged on the hem.

She looked down at me. "What?"

"You are so goddamn sexy."

"Zach…" A blush bloomed on her cheeks.

"I mean it." There was something about seeing her in my clothes that was a huge turn-on. It was probably some primal, caveman-type instinct. My hand went up the shirt to tease at the edge of her panties.

"Noooo," she moaned, but her body swayed closer to me as I slipped a finger under the elastic and found her hot, damp center.

"Yes."

Her eyes darkened to navy as she looked down at

me. "I have to get up and go to the couch before Payton wakes up," she protested.

"Then we'd better be quick and quiet."

She rolled her eyes. "Two things that you suck at."

"Wow, Emma. Way to make a man feel inadequate."

"Believe me, you are not—*gasp*—inadequate."

Two of my fingers were now buried deep in her. "I can do quick and quiet," I promised. "Come closer."

She bit her lip, eying me with suspicion, but her hips tilted toward me. I curled my fingers inside her, like I was beckoning her back to my bed.

"Oh my god," she cried out.

"Now who's being loud?"

Emma reached out to playfully slap me on the shoulder, but instead ended up clutching on to me as she rode my hand to orgasm. As she flopped onto the bed again, panting, I looked over at the clock.

"See? Six minutes, and I didn't say a fucking word. Now you, on the other hand—"

"Oh, shut up." Her voice was muffled by the blanket she'd fallen face first into. When she lifted her head and looked back over her shoulder at me, her eyes were bright and her cheeks pink. "Now I have to change my underwear again."

I said nothing, just sat up against the headboard and reached under the sheet for my aching cock. My eyes squeezed shut briefly as I wrapped my fist around it. When I opened them, Emma was kneeling in front of me on the bed with a hungry expression on her face. Her gaze flickered between the sheet bunched at my waist and the old alarm clock on the bedside table.

"Six minutes is the time to beat, huh?"

Her voice made me harder, if that was possible. She pulled back the sheet, then lowered her head over me.

"Oh fuck, baby. I love your hot, little mouth."

Apparently, we couldn't risk a morning quickie, because we knew that Payton could bust into the room, but we were okay with doing time trials for mutual sexual favors. Either way, it would be hard to explain if we were interrupted.

I let out a moan as her tongue slid over me, close to the edge already.

Maybe it was how my arousal built up while I pleasured Emma or maybe it was the heart-rattling risk of getting caught, but it didn't take long for me to come down her pretty throat. Soon, I lay there panting with my eyes closed, trying to recover.

"I win," she whispered in my ear.

"I think," I said drowsily, "that says more about me than about you."

She laughed as she left the room, and I fell back asleep.

~

"*D*ance class is the last one for the day, right?" I asked, taking the cup of coffee that Emma handed me.

"Mmmhmm." Payton nodded, her mouth full of cereal, then looked to Emma for confirmation.

"Yep."

"So, I'll pick you two up then." We'd gotten into a routine where Anderson would drop the girls off while I went to work, and then I'd pick them up after I was done. "Just text me when you're ready."

While Emma showered quickly, Payton helped me clean up the breakfast table. Well, she watched me clean up while she told me every detail of the dream she'd had about going to Disneyland on Ethan's bunkbed.

"I'm just happy that there are no more nightmares," I commented once Payton stopped talking.

She grinned. "It's because I'm not sad anymore."

My smile widened. "Really?"

Payton's eyes were bright with delight. "Yes! Well, I'm still sad that I don't get to see Mommy and Daddy but I'm just happy that I have the two of you. Mommy always told me to be thankful with what you have, no matter what."

For the hundredth time, I silently thanked Maggie for doing such an amazing job raising her daughter for the past five years. I just hoped I could do the same thing and pick up where she and Dean left off.

When I was ready to leave, I found Emma braiding Payton's hair in the living room. "See you later, sweets," I told my niece, kissing the top of her head. "That looks really pretty."

Then I turned to Emma, and I had to stop myself from kissing her as well. It was a reflex that was becoming harder to resist with every day—and night— that passed. "Bye, Emma. Take good care of her for me."

"Don't I always?" Emma asked, biting her lip. So fucking tempting…

"Oh, just kiss already."

Both Emma and I turned to see Payton smirking. "You two give each other the sneaky looks I see Daddy give Mommy and I know what it means."

My eyebrows rose. "What does it mean?"

"That you want to kiss Emma!" Payton answered in a 'duh' tone.

I bent down to stage whisper in Payton's ear, "Do you think Emma wants to kiss me?" I snuck a sideways glance at the lady in question, who was turning pink and pretending not to hear us.

"Hmmm." Payton looked from me to Emma then back to me again. "You could try it and see?"

"Good idea."

When she gave me a conspiratorial nod, I had to press my lips together to not bust out laughing.

I turned to Emma, grabbed her face, and planted a big kiss on her lips. I rested my forehead against hers. "I'll see you later, beautiful."

At the front door, I looked back to see Payton give me a big thumbs up.

There was a bubble of happiness in my chest all the way to the field, something I hadn't felt in… maybe never. Even training was going well, and we were getting ready for the season to start. Coach Matthews had been integrating me into practice and actually using my talents, which made him smart and me happy.

Payton could be credited for some of that, too. She'd told him the last time she was here that she wanted to see me play and in order for me to play, I needed to practice. So, no more endless laps and days spent in the weight room and not on the field.

Seriously, the kid was angel sent. I was reminded of that again later that afternoon in the locker room.

"Hey, Pennington!"

I'd just showered and was scrubbing a towel over my head when I heard my name. "Yeah?"

"Bring Payton around, would ya?" One of the guys

said as he pulled on a new t-shirt. "I told my kid about her and she wants to meet her."

"Uh, okay." I'd never set up a play date before. Emma usually handled that stuff.

"I know, I sound like a fucking soccer mom," he said with a chuckle. "But the truth is that players' kids don't make friends so easy. It's not the kids—it's the parents."

I nodded, understanding.

"Brianna's coming for a visit on Friday afternoon so if you bring Payton with you, they could play."

"Sure."

As I left, I had a shit-eating grin on my face at the fact that I'd just done something downright… parental. I felt proud—like I'd turned a corner or something.

Dean was probably up in heaven, laughing his ass off at me.

Now I just had to pick up Payton and Emma from dance class and go buy school supplies. I hadn't told Emma, but I was kind of stoked about it. As a kid I'd loved picking out new binders and lunchboxes and all that shit. The last time I'd done something like that, I'd been with my big brother. Now I'd get to do it with his daughter.

Dean was *definitely* laughing his ass off at me, now.

I looked up and chuckled as I gave the sky my middle finger. "Fuck you, man," I said softly. Recently I'd had more moments like that—allowing myself to be happy instead of mournful or resentful.

The summer had gone by so damn fast, with so many changes to my life that it had been kind of a blur. Even now, I realized I had time to kill because I'd rushed through getting out of the stadium. So, I decided to stop and pick up a small stuffed dog for Payton.

She'd been on a puppy campaign for the past few weeks, and Emma had shot her down as gently as possible. Privately, she'd told me that if I dared to get Payton a dog for her birthday, I'd be cleaning up the mess by myself. Payton and I were still working on her, which was one of the reasons I decided to buy Emma some flowers, too.

I parked my car at the dance studio and leaned against it as I waited for the two of them to come out. The moment she spotted me Payton ran ahead.

"Don't run in the parking lot!" I heard Emma yell at her, but my arms were already full of my niece.

"Hey, sweets! Good class?"

She showed me some new move with her leg as Emma caught up, holding her dance bag and looking a little frazzled.

"Honey, you can't run into the parking lot like that."

"Sorry," Payton said, all her focus on the movement of her outstretched leg.

I tugged on the bag, pulling Emma toward me. "To be fair, she was barely in the parking lot."

She rolled her eyes. "Only because she practically sprinted when she saw you," she grumbled, but she let me pull her closer and kiss her.

So. Goddamn. Happy.

When I lifted my head from hers, I saw Payton watching us with undisguised interest. Time to redirect her attention. "I have something for you, Pay."

Her eyes brightened with excitement and it warmed my heart. "What? What is it?"

"Close your eyes," I said, brushing my palm against her eyes to make sure that she wasn't peeking. Emma was giggling behind her as I grabbed the tiny stuffed dog that was in the car. "Okay now, open."

Payton squealed in delight the moment she saw the dog and hugged it close to her heart. "It's so soft!" she said, rubbing it against her cheek. "Thank you!"

"You're welcome, sweets."

I loved the fact that she was thrilled with the little gift and how excited she was to play with it. She immediately christened the toy Mr. Doodley and introduced it to Emma.

"It's exactly the kind I want, too! In real life," she added.

I just blinked innocently as Emma smirked at me. "Nice," she muttered under her breath at me. "Cheap move, Pennington." To Payton she just said, "Let's see how we do with Mr. Doodley first, okay?"

Yeah, we were wearing her down. As I helped Payton into her booster seat, I winked at her and got a tiny fist bump in return.

When Emma got into her seat, she was surprised to see the bouquet of tulips sitting on her spot. She looked at me and I simply smiled and shrugged. "I got Payton a little present, so I thought I'd get you one as well."

"Thanks, Zach, I love them."

When she brought the flowers close to her nose to smell them, the expression on her face was remarkably like Payton's from a couple of minutes before. As I started the car, Emma leaned over to kiss me on the cheek. I turned my head at the last minute and caught her lips, instead. And didn't let go.

Payton fake gagged in the backseat, and we broke apart.

It was school supply time. Emma had the list of

what Payton needed and all I did was push the cart and point out shit I thought looked good. Up and down the aisles, Payton asked questions about starting school. When she told me that she was excited to see Ethan more often, I suddenly had a sinking feeling. It took about six feet for my imagination to take me from their little kid sleepovers to further down the road. The mere thought made me shudder in fear.

"Why do you have that look on your face?" Emma asked as we waited for our turn to pay.

I leaned closer to her and confided, "I just thought of how I'll have to give Payton 'the talk.'"

Emma burst out laughing and hit my shoulder. "Why are you thinking that far down the line?"

I shrugged and sighed. "I don't know. I'm just not looking forward to it. You'll have to help me, or Ethan will run the risk of being punched in the nuts someday."

Something flashed in her eyes, but she remained silent and simply smiled. We paid for everything on the list—and then some—then voted to grab dinner on the way home. About halfway home, Emma dozed off. Guess staying up late and then waking up too early finally took its toll on her.

"Thanks for today… Daddy," said a small voice from the back seat.

Daddy.

Thank god I was at a red light, or I might have run off the road. I spun in my seat to look at Payton, who was still mouthing the word to herself as though trying it on like a new dress.

She smiled at me shyly and said, "Can I call you Daddy sometimes, Uncle Zach?"

"Sweets, I…" *Shit.* I didn't know what to say.

Payton sighed, sinking in her seat and explaining, "I know you're my uncle. It's just sometimes I hear other kids talking about stuff and I miss Mommy and Daddy. You and Emma could be my Daddy Two and Mommy Two or something…"

I watched her carefully as she stared out of the window, a little frown creasing her forehead. Wisps of her hair were falling out of the braid that Emma had done that morning, and my heart swelled with love for her.

"I'd be honored to have you call me Daddy, Payton," I said seriously. "I think being your dad was the best job my brother ever had."

"I guess you have the job now." Her tone was matter of fact instead of sad.

Maybe we were all adjusting. Part of me *hated* that we were all adjusting. I sent another silent "fuck you" up to heaven, but without a laugh behind it. Someone leaned on their horn behind me, and I saw the light had turned green while I was having one of the biggest moments of my life.

But then the biggest moments in life usually didn't take more time than the change of a traffic light, did they? My parents dying. Hearing my name called in the draft. Losing Maggie, then Dean. Gaining Payton. Meeting Emma.

As we continued the drive home, Payton asked, "Do you think Emma would let me call her Mommy?"

I glanced at the sleeping woman beside me and then at Payton in the rearview mirror. "I think that would make her really happy, actually." I was also ninety-nine percent certain it would also make her cry.

"Okay."

My heart suddenly ached for my little girl in the back seat. It had been too fucking soon for her to lose the people she should've been relying on for support. But I was thankful for the fact that she had faced the storm as bravely as she did. I parked the car and gently woke up Emma and the three of us headed inside the house that we all called home.

Emma helped Payton shower as I watched TV and waited for bedtime story and tuck-in time. When they got out of the bathroom, I could see Emma's eyes brimming with tears and I knew that Payton just asked her if it would be okay to call her Mommy.

For Emma's whole life she didn't have anyone to call that. While she might say that she doesn't miss it, sure as hell she never wanted another kid to feel what she had. Now here she was, becoming the Mommy that Payton needed.

We took our time going through the bedtime routine with Payton, almost reluctant to leave her to sleep. In our bedroom I wrapped my arms around Emma and pulled her close to me. She rested her forehead against my chest, her whole body sagging in a giant, shuddering sigh.

"Did you know about that?" she asked quietly.

"It came up in the car while you were sleeping." We sat together silently for a moment, my hand smoothing up and down her back. I kissed her ear, then murmured in it, "Thanks for allowing her to call you Mommy."

"I should thank her," she whispered. "She has no idea how happy she made me when she did."

We went to bed like an old married couple, quietly and comfortably. No seduction, no passion, just... together. Despite her nap in the car, Emma fell asleep immediately and I stared at her for a moment, memorizing every detail of her face.

Being faced with raising Payton was scary as hell, but now I wouldn't give it up for anything in the world —if for no other reason that it brought Emma to us. With each passing day, my feelings for both of them deepened and spread.

It made me think that on a day like today, when my balloon of happiness was stretched so thin I thought it would pop, it would still withstand whatever wind came along.

If this was love, then I guess now I can say that I know what it is.

EMMA

I knew I stepped on the line when I first slept with Zach. You know, that line between wise and foolish, boss and employee, lust and love.

Sure, I could have taken a step back and told him that it was a one-time thing, never to be repeated. In fact, I'd tried to do that—for about ninety seconds. Truth be told, after that second night my attempts to avoid being naked with Zach were kind of half-assed.

It was more fun to be whole-assed with him.

Nope, I had practically slingshot myself over the line, arcing so far that I couldn't see it behind me.

I had allowed myself to tumble down the rabbit hole and I wasn't even sure if Zach was willing to catch me at the end of it or if he even was waiting for me.

Sleeping with Zach Pennington with no feelings attached would've been much easier if we didn't see each other every single day and didn't have a kid who called us Mommy and Daddy. Payton wasn't our child, but she sure acted like she was, and seeing the way Zach and she interacted nowadays made me fall for him even more.

So, I'd overstepped. I'd flown high and tumbled down. And now I'd fallen.

Anyone in their right mind would say that I needed some physical therapy.

It only takes getting your heart broken once to be reluctant to risk it again. The thing about the heart, though, is that it's a damn strong muscle. If there's a battle between your heart and your brain, odds are your heart will win out—which is why I was looking back at that *line* and wondering where it went.

The thing was, I was no stranger to heartbreak. I felt it when I was young, when my parents died and that was probably the worst heartbreak one could ever go through.

Heartbreak meant loving, then losing.

If Zach Pennington was to break my heart, he wasn't the only person I'd lose in the process. It meant that I would lose Payton too. Not only did I not want to put her through that kind of pain, I didn't want to face it either. Unfortunately, part of what we had in common was knowing what that kind of pain felt like already. All three of us had lost our parents when we were young. It was a strange kind of club. The dues were astronomical.

But if Payton lost me then that meant she lost her mom—twice—in less than a year.

"You know it's not healthy to be that buried in your thoughts, right?"

I looked up and met Anderson's warm hazel eyes and smiled slightly. "It's nothing, Andy."

"Tell that to the line in your forehead," he said, sipping a chai latte as we waited for Payton finish her piano lessons. Zach's assistant and I had spent enough time together that we'd developed a friendship—maybe the first real one that I'd had in my life.

I pressed my fingers to my head. Was there really a wrinkle there? "No, it's really nothing."

He put down the tablet on which he'd been maneuvering Zach's schedule for the month, then looked at me with a glint in his eye. "I'm pretty sure that it has something to do with Zach Pennington and how he managed to make you drop your panties within three days of you living with him."

My eyes widened and I immediately shushed him, looking around the café to see if anyone had heard what Andy had said. I glared at him and leaned back on my chair, crossing my arms against my chest. "You know that's not true."

"Okay, a week."

I opened my mouth, then closed it again.

He chuckled. "Oh, but you don't deny that Zach had filled your thoughts and not just…" He glanced down, making me blush and slap at his hand on the table.

"Andy, you're not really helping here. You're supposed to be my friend."

And Zach's employee, like I was. This is how things got messed up. Was he Zach's assistant first and my friend second? Was Zach my employer first and my lover second?

Anderson laughed. "How am I supposed to help when I don't even know what your dilemma is?"

I sighed and then played with my hands. "I just didn't think…"

"That you'd fall hard and fast for Zach Pennington and not just on the bed?" Andy finished for me.

He was right. I didn't like it, but I had to concede that it was true. I didn't expect—didn't *plan* to sleep with my boss, but I had. And god knows that I never planned or expected to fall in love with him, too.

"What's the problem, Em?"

"The problem is I like Zach more than I'm supposed to," I began to say, "and if I get rejected or if he breaks my heart, I don't think I could be around him anymore." I sighed. "Which means I would have to leave Payton." It was a double whammy.

"And you love that kid too much," Andy said, looking at me understandingly, "We all do."

I nodded. "I don't know what to do, Andy."

"Why not ask Zach where you stand in his life?" Andy suggested, tilting his head at me. "I've never seen him as happy as he is now, Emma. It's not just Payton that makes him happy. I think it's you, too."

My phone buzzed before I could respond. I looked down at the text message, then up at Anderson again. "Do you really think I should ask him that?"

He nodded. "Yes. Yes, I do. I think you'd be pleasantly surprised."

"Okay." I took a deep breath. Maybe I needed him with me, but not for moral support. No, I needed him to kick me in the ass.

"Okay, what?"

"Looks like Payton's art class is cancelled. What do you say we pay Zach a surprise visit?"

"I say 'surprise!'"

Once her piano lesson was over, Payton was more than happy to be in on the plan. Her delight threatened to ruin the surprise, though, as she was so excited that she ran to the minivan, announcing to anyone in earshot that she was going to the field to see her Daddy.

She loved going to the football field where Zach trained. She'd become a kind of miniature mascot for the team. They would play catch with her and she would run around the field like a crazed kid—which, incidentally, she was—and Zach's teammates would chase her. It was a novel kind of workout and a fun sight to watch, especially when they tried to teach her to play football. Nothing made him happier than having the chance to teach her the sport that he loved.

It was obvious to anyone watching that he would make a great father to his own kids someday. I couldn't help but wish that I'd be along for the ride.

When we arrived at the stadium, Payton was so excited she hopped out of the car the moment Anderson parked. I had to chase after her, but I didn't mind. I was just as excited as she was.

I caught up to her sooner than I expected, since she couldn't get past the entrance. Before her eyes and above her head was a wall of people with flashing cameras and barking voices. Reporters? I shook my head, trying to recall if Zach had said anything about a press conference that morning. No, these visitors weren't welcome. The security guards were irritably fending them off and Zach's coach stood behind them, his face red with annoyance.

"Coach!" Payton screamed and tried to squeeze her way past the paparazzi.

"Payton!" My eyes widened as she disappeared into the crowd. I panicked when couldn't see her for all the people pushing and shoving. My heart only slowed down again when I squirmed in to find her clinging to Coach Matthews.

Matthews yelled something at a guard, then led the three of us inside.

"What's going on?" I asked the moment we were away from the crowd. I looked back to see Anderson being let through by one of the guards, jogging down the concourse to catch up with us.

"Some celebrity chick just dropped by with the paparazzi hot on her tail," Coach grumbled.

"Celebrity?" Anderson repeated once we got on the field. There was a strange tone in his voice, one I'd never heard before.

The team appeared to be in a huddle, but there was a gorgeous woman in the middle instead of a football. She looked like a movie star or something. Everyone's attention was on her, and it appeared from the expression on her face that that was what she'd came for. What she expected.

But not Payton.

"Daddy!" she screamed as she rushed to Zach.

It was only then that I spotted the tangle of cables in her path.

It was as if everything happened in slow-motion as I ran to Payton, but she sprinted faster than I ever could and her excitement to see her uncle only fueled her adrenaline. I watched helplessly as she tripped and hit the cement. *Hard*.

"Shit!" My heart stopped the moment I spotted blood. "Payton!" I screamed, and it was a race to see who could get to her first.

Zach was the first to reach her. He cradled her in his arms, his face drained of color. Payton was barely conscious, and though common sense told me not to touch her head I couldn't help but want to stop the blood oozing from it. In the background I heard someone calling an ambulance, and I felt like I was going to be sick from shock.

Finally, the paramedics arrived. They let Zach ride in the ambulance with Payton, but not me. I was nearly wild with fear and fury, and only Anderson was able to yank me away and propel me to the car to make our own way to the hospital. When we met them in the ER, Zach was struggling to answer questions about Payton's medical history.

Activity swirled around us like a sandstorm in the desert, and all too quickly we were left in the waiting room as they rushed Payton to surgery. A nurse told us where to wait, and my knees felt like they were going to give out if I didn't find a chair. Zach paced in front of us as Anderson sat beside me, glued to his phone.

About ten minutes into our wait, someone came into the room. We all looked up with anticipation, only to be glared at by the woman from the field. Her sunglasses masked her expression, but her glossy lips were set into a thin line and she marched in like she owned the place.

"Zachary!"

I flinched as she said Zach's name. When she slapped him, I sprang to my feet and stared at them in shock.

"You have a daughter? You never told me you had a daughter!"

"What the hell, Camille?" Zach said, glaring at her.

"What do you mean, 'what the hell, Camille'? You're the one who didn't tell his girlfriend that he had a daughter. When were you planning on telling me, Zach? Before or after I moved to Denver?"

Her head whipped around to take in her audience, and it was only then that I recognized who she was—sultry Latina movie starlet Camille Mendez. She had a reputation for melodrama, on and off the screen, but men panted after her regardless. Including Zach Pennington, apparently.

"Are you the kid's mother?" she said, sneering at me. "Oh god, Zachary, did you even get that kid's blood tested? She might not even be yours. I mean, look at this girl. She might have fucked you just to trick you into supporting another man's child."

"Hey!" Now Anderson was on his feet beside me, and my head reared back as though she'd slapped me, as well.

Compared to her, I was nothing.

Compared to her beauty, her fame, her personality and lifestyle, I was nothing.

I was merely Payton's nanny and if she was Zach's girlfriend, like she said she was, then I had... nothing.

All I could do was stare at Zach, knowing that my heart's pain was reflected in my eyes. I felt numb, unsure of what I was supposed to do or say. I heard Anderson say Zach's name, and I think he took my hand.

I cleared my throat and sniffed deeply to hold my tears in as I met Camille's contemptuous assessment head-on.

"I'm Payton's nanny," I said, my voice hoarse.

Camille raised an eyebrow, looking between me and Zach. "Oh, that's priceless. Zachary, please tell me you haven't been fucking the help. I'm willing to forgive a lot of things—*obviously*—but leading this poor, dumb girl on…" She clucked her tongue, whether in sympathy for me or disdain for him, I wasn't sure.

"Camille!" I heard Zach's voice but couldn't take my eyes off his fiery girlfriend.

She pinned me in place with a curled lip. "Sweetheart, he's out of your league. Just… don't even bother trying." She lowered her voice, like she was sharing a secret with me. "You're embarrassing him."

So, it was sympathy for him and disdain for me.

"Camille, that's enough," he snapped.

"Jesus, Zachary," she groaned, "why didn't you just give her money? Or get her to terminate? Now we're going to have to deal with this!" She stomped her foot on the worn linoleum, her stiletto briefly threatening to skid underneath her. "And I've got a four-month shoot coming up!"

Then she turned to me, her lips pouting with fake sincerity. "I'm sorry he led you on like this. But whatever he promised you—"

"He didn't promise me anything," I said quietly. "And you're right. He is out of my league, and I've known that from the start. I… made a mistake."

I spun around and dashed out of the room like I needed emergency surgery myself. I heard Zach calling my name angrily behind me, but I got to the exit before he could catch up. When I emerged into the parking lot, I looked around for a bus stop sign or something.

I couldn't breathe. I could feel pieces of my heart falling off and shattering.

Oh, I'd been so wrong. This was so much worse than any other heartbreak. I was losing Payton and Zach, and I had nobody to blame but myself. And Payton wasn't even conscious. I swayed when I thought of her alone on the operating table upstairs.

"Emma!"

Anderson was panting by the time he finally reached me. "Emma, c'mon, don't leave like that."

I shook my head. "No. I messed up, Andy. This is my fault. I shouldn't have slept with Zach. I shouldn't have fallen in love with him. I can't do this."

"What do you mean?"

"I'm quitting," I whispered, knowing that the two words hurt me more than Zach's lies because it meant that I wouldn't see Payton again.

"Emma, what about Payton? You can't leave her." Andy tried to reason with me, tried to talk some sense into me, but I was too filled with pain and heartache to think straight. "Emma, just listen, okay? I can explain everything about Camille."

I shook my head, refusing to be fed more lies. Anderson was Zach's assistant and even though he was my friend, his loyalty should still be to his boss.

"No, Andy. It's okay. I shouldn't have hoped. This is where hope leads us to anyways. It always leads to heartbreak and who am I kidding? Camille's right. Zach's way out of my league. I'm just another good lay for him."

The bus arrived and I turned to it, waving at the driver to tell him that I just needed a moment. I looked back to Andy.

"I'll get my things at the house and then I'll be out of your hair before you even know it. If Payton looks for me…"

I paused, trying to compose myself. This would break Payton's heart, but I couldn't stay with the knowledge that she'd be living in the crossfire of tension and drama between Zach and me. Once again, I hated myself for crossing the line knowing that this would affect Payton too.

"Tell her that I love her and that I'll visit her in her classes sometimes but I'm sorry, I can't take care of her anymore." A tear rolled down my cheek. "You can settle everything with the agency, Andy. I'll give them the heads up and let them know that the conflict was on my end. And I guess this is goodbye."

ZACH

*M*y head was spinning so hard I thought I'd throw up.

Nothing today made sense.

Camille came to Denver, which was something that I never truly expected from her. I broke it off with her before Dean even died and I thought I'd been firm about it this time. And I thought that since I came to Denver, she wouldn't have the chance find me and throw herself at me.

Back in Florida, Camille had been my on and off girlfriend. She was more off than on, in the past year. Sometimes I'd tire of her and then I'd break it off, or sometimes she'd find me locking lips with a girl I met at a club or a fan willing to throw herself at me for a one-night stand. But even after all of those things, Camille always came back. She'd date other guys, but in the end, she always came back to me. And I to her.

It was fun when I was back in Florida. She was like an on-call lay when I didn't feel like going out. But it was different now. I was different now.

It was different because I had Emma. And Payton.

Finally, the doctor came to talk to us about Payton's surgery. When he appeared in the doorway, I recognized him as the same one who broke the news to me about Dean's condition. The sight of him made my heart ache, my worry for my niece getting ten times worse. I pushed past Camille, blatantly ignoring her.

He looked at me and gave me a nod of acknowledgment. "Hello, Mr. Pennington."

"How's my niece?"

When I said the word niece, I heard Camille gasp behind me. No matter how furious she was, it was nothing to how much I wanted to slap her upside the head.

She caused a scene for nothing. She demeaned Emma for nothing. I wanted to scream at her earlier when Emma ran off but right then the doctor appeared, and I needed to know that Payton was alright before I went to search for Emma and explain everything to her.

"She's in good condition. We were able to reduce the hematoma. Still in recovery and unconscious, but she'll be fine, Zach," he assured me. "We're watching her for concussion symptoms, but she can probably go home tomorrow. But no more football without a helmet," he said with a gentle smile. The fact that he was joking filled me with true relief.

"Can I see her?" I asked.

He nodded. "Yes. I'll have someone come and tell you when they're transferring her to a room. In the meantime, I'm sure you probably have some more forms to fill out for Admitting."

Camille didn't like being ignored, but that's what happened for the next hour. Honestly, I was surprised that she hung around that long. I probably should have told her to leave, but I couldn't care enough to bother.

I got to Payton's room as they were just wheeling her in, so I stood back and let them do their job. Once in the bed, she looked so small and pale. I couldn't help but think about the last time I saw her in a hospital bed, when our worlds had just fell apart.

"Oh, sweets." I sank onto the chair beside my niece, reaching for her hand. I laced my fingers with hers, mindful of her IV line. "You scared the shit out of me," I murmured.

When Anderson returned, Emma wasn't with him. "Where the fuck have you been?" I snapped at him.

He frowned at Camille, who was standing on the other side of the room looking uncomfortable.

My eyebrows furrowed. I knew that what Camille had said to her had stung, but I thought she was stronger than that. I expected her to bounce back and ignore Camille's bitchiness, because Payton was hurt and Payton was the one who mattered.

"Where's Emma?" I asked him.

He looked at me helplessly and shrugged, but there was a hardness in his eyes that I'd never seen before.

Camille snorted. "Why are you looking for the nanny, anyways? The kid has nurses now."

I closed my eyes and rubbed my palm against my face. "Why are you still here, Camille?"

I heard the click of her heels on the floor and opened my eyes to see her sashaying over to me, batting her lashes.

"Because we belong together, Zach," Camille said, perching on my lap and wrapping her arms around my neck like a snake. "I realized that what I feel for you is true and sure and that I would never feel that way about anyone else."

Ha! I knew her game. Her latest rendezvous didn't work out, and now she needed someone who would accept her with open arms and make her feel she was wanted. I'd never been one for relationships, but I play-acted well with Camille, pretending I cared when I didn't.

I shook my head and pushed her off of me, laughing at her humourlessly. "God, Camille, I know you're not really this stupid. I'm done with this, okay?"

"You've said that before," Camille reminded me, staring right into my eyes, "but the moment you see me naked, you throw me on the bed and fuck me."

I rolled my eyes. "Because you come into my apartment wearing nothing beneath your coat. But I'm not that man anymore, Camille. And watch your fucking language around Payton."

My heart began to beat double-time as Payton began to stir. Camille squawked as I stood up suddenly, grabbed her wrist and dragged her out of the room before Payton saw her.

She pulled her arm roughly out of my grasp and rubbed her wrist. "What did that kid do to you? You've changed."

"Yeah, I have. That kid is my family. We need each other," I told Camille. "Look, I'm sorry I ever agreed to play this game with you. I'm sorry for making you think that you always have someone to come back to with me, but I'm done."

"But you—"

"I'm *done*. I'm done with the game, I'm done with your dramatic crap, and I'm done with *you*."

I knew that my words stung but I could only hope that it got through to her. She could've stripped off her clothes in front of me in public and not care, as long as she got my attention.

"Camille, please. My niece needs me. She needs a father and I'm that person for her."

"You could be her father and you could still be my man."

I smiled sadly at her. "That's the thing. I'm also someone else's man."

Camille stood dumbfounded in front of me and I sighed. "I didn't think I'd fall in love, Cam. Trust me—I liked the playboy games. And you're right, I could continue fucking girls and be the father that Payton needs, but right now I simply want to be her father and be someone's man. No games."

"Who?" Camille seethed, her eyes narrowing. "The *nanny*? You want to be with her? Oh, for God's sake, Zachary, you are way out of her league!"

I rolled my eyes. "Actually, *she's* way out of *my* league. And if you value your fame, I suggest you leave now. Anderson's probably calling TMZ right now."

Camille scoffed, but I saw her eyes widen with alarm. "Don't expect that I'm gonna accept you when you come crawling back to me."

"I'm counting on it," I replied. "Goodbye, Camille."

I watched to make sure that she really left, then went back to Payton's room to find her awake and crying. I rushed to her side. "Sweets, how are you feeling?"

Payton looked at me with her big brown eyes brimming with tears. "Where's Emma? I want Emma!"

I looked at Anderson, who looked like he didn't know what he was going to do. I remembered he chased after Emma while I tried to handle Camille and waited for the doctor to tell me about Payton's condition.

Anderson looked at me and then nodded at the door. I turned to Payton. "Give me and Andy a minute, okay? I'll find out where Emma is."

The two of us headed out of the door and I crossed my arms, looking at him. "Where is she?"

"She went home to pack her things," Anderson told me in a defeated voice. "She says she's done, Zach."

"What does you mean, she's done?" I asked. What was he even talking about?

"I don't know!" Anderson said. "Look, if you rush now, you might still find her there. She took the bus to get there and I know that the ride there must take her half an hour. Get there quick, Zach, and try to talk her out of it."

I was ready to run to the exit when Anderson called my name again. I stopped and turned to him. "What?"

"She told me she's in love with you," Anderson said, a small smile on his face. "I thought you should know. And here are the keys. Might help you out."

It was as if something was switched on inside of me. I sprinted to the hospital parking lot and found the minivan in less than five minutes. I drove to the house at top speed, praying to whatever god who was listening that I would still find Emma there.

My prayers were answered.

The moment I parked the car, Emma came out of the house.

I rushed to her. "Emma!"

She hesitated, her eyes red and puffy. She had been crying. Why had she been crying? Did she honestly believe Camille's lies?

I held her face in my hands, staring straight into the beautiful blue eyes that I'd fallen in love with. She looked away and placed a hand on mine, pushing mine away weakly.

"Emma, don't go."

It was all I could think of saying. I could've told her I'd fallen in love with her, but I didn't know how. I didn't know what I was supposed to say or how to even start the confession. All I wanted was for her to stay.

"You can't go."

But she shook her head. "I've had enough of this, Zach."

"Enough of what? Of me and Payton?"

She looked at me, her eyes sad and defeated. "What am I to you?"

What did she mean? She was the girl I was in love with. But my mouth refused to open and my voice suddenly disappeared. All I could do was stare at her as she closed her eyes and looked down.

"Camille was right. We don't... fit together, and I shouldn't have crossed the line. It was unprofessional of me," she choked out. "It's all my fault."

"No, it's not. Look, Emma, just put your things back in the house and we'll talk about this, okay?" I said, trying to reason with her.

She shook her head. Damn it, why was she being so stubborn? Didn't she know she belonged here with us?

"I don't want you to go. Payton doesn't want you to go. She was crying when she woke up and you weren't there."

"Payton's a strong girl. She'll get through this," Emma said, trying to sound convincing. I wasn't sure who she was convincing though—me or her. Payton may be stronger than both of us put together, but what about me? I needed her.

But I didn't know how to say it.

I reached out to take her hand in mine, looking at our fingers entwined together. Dean always told me that Maggie completed him, like his whole life had begun as pieces of puzzles that he had tried to piece together unsuccessfully—until Maggie came along with the missing piece. Dean told me that was what love felt like.

Emma completed me too. I just didn't know how I was supposed to tell her that.

I squeezed her hand tightly in mine. "*I* want you to stay."

When she looked at me, I saw a war being waged inside her. She wanted to stay. I could see it in her eyes and feel it in her touch. What was stopping her?

"Give me a reason, Zach."

I could have said that I was in love with her at that moment. I should have professed my feelings for her right then and there.

Emma looked away again and pulled her hand from my grasp. She adjusted her bag on her shoulders and looked down at her feet.

"I love Payton, Zach. I would still like to see her some time, even if I'm no longer her nanny," she said, her voice cracking. "I'll make sure you get a good nanny for her, Zach."

She grabbed her luggage and walked past me. I stood still, my heart racing as though I was playing the last down of a tied game—only that felt like it would be easier to win.

All I needed to do was confess, to turn around and tell her how I felt about her. So what if everyone I loved,

I ended up losing? Wasn't there a poem or something about that being a good thing? I wasn't under a curse, so why was I acting like admitting I love someone was like a death knell?

"Emma!" I spun around to face her. I couldn't stand the idea of watching her walk away from our home. It took everything inside me to blurt out, "I need you."

"For what, Zach?" Her voice rose with frustration as she turned back again. "An easy lay? A good cook and babysitter?"

"No!" She wasn't any of those things. No, wait, she *was* a good cook and babysitter, but damned if I would let her put words in my mouth that I didn't say. I strode ahead to where she stood on the front walk, but she held up a palm to stop me.

"Then what am I to you?" she demanded again. "If I fall, are you willing to catch me? Are you willing to make this be more than just stolen moments when Payton's asleep? Are you willing to make it real between us, for all of us? Because—call me a fool—I am. I want it to be real. I want you, Zachary Pennington, more than I ever wanted anyone my whole life."

"Then why won't you stay?"

"Because I know what it feels like when the other person doesn't want you. I've felt that way for a majority of my life, Zach, transferring from foster home to foster home. No matter how hard I tried to make them like me so I could stay, no one did."

"But I'm different. Payton and I, we could be home to you. You would be safe, happy, not have to work too hard—"

Something flashed in Emma's eyes. "I'm not a puppy, Zach." She sighed, tucking in a stray strand of hair. "Tell me why I should stay. Just give me one good reason and I would."

But I couldn't. I couldn't say a damn thing. I wanted to tell her I love her and that it was all the reason she needed, but for some reason I just stood there like an idiot.

"Maybe you've taken too many hits to the head," Emma muttered, closing her eyes briefly and frowning.

"What?"

Then she inhaled deeply, placed a hand on my shoulder and squeezed it lightly. "I hope you continue being the father that you're being to Payton, Zach. She needs it. So do you," she added softly. Her fingertips landed on my lips so briefly I wondered if maybe I'd imagined it.

She'd made it to the Uber that I hadn't noticed waiting for her when I managed to call out her name again. Without responding, she loaded her bags in the trunk.

"Emma!"

She had the back door open and was about to get in. She was really going to leave. I couldn't believe it.

"Give me a chance," I pleaded.

She raised her head to look me in the eye. "I just gave you…" She threw up her hands. "God, I don't *know* how many chances!"

"But—"

"You know what, Zach? I *deserve* someone who can tell me why they want me and make it sound like more than a damn job description."

And with those words, she swept into the car and slammed the door behind her.

EMMA

I winced at the squeak of the door when I swung it open. It was like a little 'welcome back' to the dingy apartment I lived in before I was hired to be Payton's nanny. It was lucky for me that the agency got Zach slash Anderson to agree to pay to retain it for the first six months.

Lucky... right. Maybe if I looked at it from a more optimistic perspective, it wouldn't be so bad.

It wasn't cramped, it was homey.

It wasn't dingy and worn out, it had a funky, vintage vibe.

The hot water, heat and electricity weren't unreliable, they were ideal for disconnecting and getting back to nature.

I had my doubts as to how I could spin the tree roots in the pipes as "sustainable plumbing," though.

At least I had a new job already. The agency had told me about a few nanny positions, but I told them that I was burnt out of caregiving at the moment. Could they find me something... simpler?

So, now I was working at a drugstore, which was mind-numbingly boring and full of assholes every day, but at least it didn't make me cry. It paid enough for me to afford the rent, my bills, and more or less three meals a day.

And like I said, it didn't make me cry.

Anderson called me a few times. Even though he knew my quaint apartment had been retained, he still asked if I wanted to come live with him. I was sure he offered because we were friends, but I still felt like he felt bad for me.

That was what I hated most—pity. I hated it when people felt sorry for me. I was a survivor, not a charity case.

But calls with Anderson were a chance to ask about Payton and how she was doing. I was horrified to find out they had to shave part of her head to give her stitches. I could only imagine how she cried when she saw herself in the mirror, and my arms ached to hold her. She wasn't fond of scars. She hated the gashes she had on her arms from the accident, told me that it reminded her too much of what she had lost.

I hoped that the scars on her forehead wouldn't remind her of losing me now, too. That thought was like a knife twisting in my chest, not just because how I felt at losing her, but that she would feel any more heartbreak at my hands.

Sometimes I wondered: if only I was courageous enough, I would've stayed. I thought about it at night when I couldn't sleep, but by the light of dawn I realized that Zach was the one who was the coward.

The more it percolated in my mind, the more convinced I was that I was right.

All I'd wanted was the assurance and the confirmation that he felt something for me, too. I *deserved* that, and then some. I deserved a man who could tell me that he loved me, got down on his knees to worship me, list a hundred reasons why he needed me.

Okay, I'd settle for a dozen.

I was a coward in my own way, though. I couldn't face Zach. He called me more often than Anderson had, but I let his calls go straight to voicemail and then afterwards listened to him struggle to leave me a message.

As I sank down onto the worn-out sofa that came with the apartment, I felt the springs poke my backside. A self-pitying sigh escaped me. I was back to the life that I was so sure I was ready to leave behind. When Zach hired me, I thought that maybe I could afford a new apartment, better furniture… and last longer than I had as Payton's nanny.

Hell, I had teenage acne that lasted longer than my job as Payton's nanny. And the scars from that weren't nearly as bad.

But I just had to cross that line, didn't I?

My phone vibrated in my back pocket and I dug it out. It was the assistant manager of the drugstore, asking if I could come in. Not having anything better to do, or feeling like I had much of a choice, I said I'd be there in forty minutes. I just had to hop in the shower and change into my last clean uniform.

The bus dropped me off at the drugstore thirty minutes later and I saw that the assistant manager was manning the cash register and that the handful of other employees were busy doing their jobs. I pasted on a smile and took over the check-out. Honestly, I was happy to take over and allow my mind to be preoccupied with scanning items and giving change.

Until a lull came.

When the last customer left and the store became silent, I began to restock the shelves. Open the box, empty the box. I was so lost in my robotic task that I jumped when I heard the door chime. I looked up to see a little girl walk in.

I must've been so tired that I was hallucinating but the little girl looked so much like Payton that I wanted to cry. I closed my eyes, took a deep breath and swallowed the lump in my throat, and when I looked up again she'd disappeared around the corner, near the front counter.

My body aching, I straightened and walked back to the cash register, where she was looking up at the display screen. I tapped her shoulder gently and was ready to ask what it was that she needed or if she was lost.

When she turned around, I just about burst into tears.

"Mommy!"

It was really Payton. My eyes widened as she jumped into my arms. I caught her, picked her up and hugged her like she was my Mr. Doodley. She squealed with delight as her small arms wrapped around my neck.

I couldn't believe it, but it was her. She was real and warm and in my arms. After only a week, I'd already missed her enough for a lifetime.

"Oh god, I've missed you, Pay." I showered her with kisses as she giggled, holding onto me tightly.

Her bright eyes shone at me, the fluorescent light overhead blurring around her hair like a halo. "I missed you too. You shouldn't have gone away," she scolded me.

I wasn't sure how to explain to her that "Daddy was an emotional scaredy-cat."

"How have you been?" I asked her. I set her down and knelt before her. My arms steadied her as she leaned into me.

"I don't like the stitches."

I nodded, figuring as much.

"But I didn't like you leaving even more."

I smoothed her hair down and held her face gently with my hands. "I'm so sorry, Payton. I never wanted to leave you." That was the honest truth.

"Why did you leave? You promised me you wouldn't," Payton said, her brown eyes holding the confusion and innocence that only a child could.

Please, twist the knife a little more, kid! "I don't know. I was scared." I stood, ashamed to admit that to her.

"Can you be *not* scared now?"

"It doesn't work that way."

"Then make it," she ordered me and then began to tug me toward the door. I stayed firmly where I stood.

"Sweetheart, I can't just leave. I have work."

"No, you don't," she said. "We've talked to them."

I laughed. She sounded like a miniature mobster. Then I realized that I'd been so caught up in Payton that I hadn't considered the fact that she couldn't have come alone.

At the pharmacist's counter, the rest of my co-workers were all back from their breaks and grinning at me. What was going on? Were they all a part of this?

Payton continued to tug at my arm and I finally relented, allowing her to drag me outside of the drugstore and to the parking lot. It was when we reached the parking lot that I saw Zach.

He stood in the middle of the lot, a bouquet in his hands. He looked like hell. He had bags under his eyes, and I thought I saw new lines carved into his tired face. It should have satisfied me on some level that he was in just as much pain as I was, but instead it just made everything hurt more.

"Hi," he said softly as we neared him. He handed Payton the bouquet he was holding and stepped closer to me.

Instinctively I turned to Payton. She only moved six feet away from us, but I was suddenly scared that a car would come.

"Don't worry," Zach said. "Anderson's here, too. He's looking out for her to make sure she's safe while we talk. I'd tell her to stay with Andy the whole time, but I know that she won't."

"What are you doing here, Zach?" I asked him.

He ran a hand through his hair, messing it up more than it already was. "I came here to talk, Emma. Beg, if I must."

"For what?"

"For you to come back to us," he answered quietly. "I meant what I said that Payton and I can be the home that you want, that you need."

I closed my eyes. His words were sweeter than any honey and candy the world could offer but sometimes even the sweetest things in the world could turn bitter and rancid when expired. "What about Camille?"

"Camille's gone. You've got it all wrong, Emma. We broke up. She's the only one caught in a bubble that we're still together. She thought if she came back, I'll just take her back like we never ended it."

"Didn't you always?" I countered, remembering all

of the articles I read online in an unfortunate fit of masochism.

Understanding flashed in Zach's eyes and he took another step closer to me. "Camille never meant anything to me. She was an easy lay."

"Wasn't I, too?" I asked, the truth of my words like a sword to my own heart.

"Never."

"I lived with you. I allowed myself to sleep with you and crossed the line. If you wanted to fuck me, I was willing to spread my legs for you because I was so stupid thinking that it could turn into something more. I was already stupid enough to have sex with you, I was even dumber to allow myself to fall in love with you. What was I thinking?"

Zach's eyebrows furrowed and he reached out to gently touch my face, then he said, "Do you think you're stupid to have fallen in love with your boss?"

"Yes," I whispered.

"Then I guess we're in the same boat. I'm stupid for falling in love with my niece's nanny, but we can't stop our hearts from what they want, can we?"

I took a step back and stared at him, his words ricocheting in my brain and to my heart. "What?"

Zach smiled sheepishly. "See, I've never fallen in love, Emma. I never allowed myself to. I was content with being a bachelor, because it was easier than getting hurt. When I lost my parents, Dean and Maggie—and Payton—became my only family. Then I just had Payton. I convinced myself that if I allowed myself to fall in love with you, chances were that I'd end up losing you, too."

I opened my mouth to say something, but Zach

shushed me with a finger on my lips. He gave me a crooked smile, the same one that made my heart melt in a puddle. Damn him for being my weakness. He was worse than chocolate.

"But no matter how we shield our hearts," he continued, "it still wants what it wants, and we can't fight that, can we?"

"Are you…?"

He chuckled and pressed his lips against my forehead gently. His brown eyes were bright with delight and I could no longer see how tired he was. "I was a mess when you left. I had to nurse a broken heart and I had to nurse an even more broken little girl. And you know, I'm no cardiologist."

I guess that explained why he looked so exhausted. "Zach, what are you trying to say?"

"What I'm trying to say is that I love you, Emma."

"Oh."

"You wanted me to give you a reason. After you left, it was all I could think about. I must have written down about a hundred reasons."

I lifted an eyebrow.

"Okay, maybe about twenty. Payton helped me brainstorm," he added.

"But there's only one that really counts, and that's why I think you should stay. Or, come back." he told me, his voice soothing and quiet to my ears.

His voice was quiet, soothing to my ears, and I leaned into him without thinking. His mouth pressed against my temple.

"I'm not good with words, Emma. I'm better with actions."

"You could use practice with both, I'd say," I muttered.

He chuckled. "I never told anyone I loved them before, so I didn't know what I was supposed to say."

I reared back to stare at him. My heart was racing, beating a mile per minute and I wanted to replay his words over and over in my head. "Huh?" Now I was the one who was speechless.

Zach laughed. "You know what? You're absolutely right. I need more practice."

He placed both of his hands on my face and then crashed his mouth against me. His lips were soft and tender against mine, cautious and waiting for my response. But I could feel it, I could feel the words that he didn't know how to say. His lips might not form the words that I needed to hear but they did perfectly well on letting me feel what he meant.

I kissed him back once everything finally sank in.

I was sure that the two of us stood there, kissing each other in the middle of the parking lot as the sun sank down, kissing the world goodbye for a few hours… just like how Zach and I were kissing each other but not goodbye. No, this was a beginning, another new chapter that the both of us had never thought we could open.

We pulled apart and he leaned forward to rest his forehead against mine, as though he couldn't truly part from me. I looked into Zach's eyes, swirls of brown bright with delight and happiness and love.

So much love.

More love than I've ever felt in my entire life. I could feel myself melting at the weight of it all.

"I love you," Zach said, his voice firm and he said it with such finality.

I wanted to say it back, to answer him with the same intensity. But there was one more thing that I needed to know. "What if you get tired of me?"

Zach smiled and tilted his head to look at me. "See, that's another thing about Penningtons that maybe I didn't tell you. My dad and brother, they only fell in love once and they married the girl."

His eyebrows waggled and I couldn't stop myself from laughing. I pushed him away playfully.

Of course, I'd dreamed of marrying the love of my life one day. Today, I felt as though that dream could become reality. And what I felt for Zach... it was one of the most real and honest things I'd felt in my entire life.

"I love you," I finally said, sinking into his body and soul. I touched his face. "I am so very in love with you, Zach Pennington."

He kissed me gently on the forehead. "That's good because you're stuck with me for a very long time, Miss Emma Smith."

If someone told me last year that I would fall in love with my boss, I would have laughed in their face and told him that it would never happen. Real life didn't turn out that way.

But I did. It did happen and I guess that's the thing about life. Just because you don't have a beautiful back-story, doesn't mean you can't have a happy ending. In fact, you might get something even better.

"Mommy!" I heard Payton scream and Zach and I pulled apart to watch her race toward us.

"No running in the parking lot!" we both yelled.

She almost fell over her own feet as she rocked to a halt. Her face fell, and I knew that she had been waiting for the moment she was close enough to jump into our arms.

"C'mere, Pay."

She walked to us slowly and cautiously. Zach snorted and I elbowed him in the stomach. "Don't laugh at her."

When she reached us, we had a big group hug. "You know, I think it's better taking it slow," she said.

My heart warmed and I looked over to where Zach stood. I could see his eyes shining with unshed tears. Who would have thought that three orphans could become each other's family?

Now *that* was a happy ending for the books.

THE END

ACKNOWLEDGMENTS

Above everything I believe writing and reading should be fun and leave you with a smile on your face, so I hope you enjoyed this book! Please consider leaving a review if you do like it, to help other readers. I know that I check out reviews before I buy books, myself.

My eternal gratitude goes out to Jessica Estep and all her colleagues at Inkslinger PR, as well as the rock stars at Give Me Books. You're all amazing—and *so patient*.

I also send psychic thanks to Amanda Walker, Vivian Tabonda and Crystal Kook on a daily basis; Angela Evans and Kristen Echo at least weekly; and the patron saint of procrastination *(reminder: look that up later to insert here)* on a shifting, semi-annual schedule.

Lastly, Dr. Kaye and my twin boys are the real heroes, for their understanding and patience. And in the case of my boys, I *really* appreciate their acceptance of my answers to questions such as "Mummy, what's porn?"

ABOUT THE AUTHOR

Nikky Kaye likes to read and write feverish, fearless books for your funny boner, such as *A Model Fiancé* and the *Billionaire Book Club* series.

A former college professor, she has worked with movie stars and the United Nations—but now prefers to deal in happy endings.

Her world revolves around her twin boys, a shameful diet cola addiction, writing, and napping. Okay, maybe napping, then writing.

For exclusive excerpts of upcoming releases, contests and other fun stuff, sign up for her Coming Attractions newsletter at

http://www.subscribepage.com/nikkykaye

www.nikkykaye.com
read@nikkykaye.com

facebook.com/officialnikkykayeauthor

instagram.com/nikkykayebooks

bookbub.com/authors/nikky-kaye

amazon.com/author/nikkykaye

www.ingramcontent.com/pod-product-compliance
Lightning Source LLC
Chambersburg PA
CBHW022030170626
46808CB00003B/1129